A MAZE OF MURDERS

A MAZE OF MURDERS

An Inspector Alvarez Novel

Roderic Jeffries

Chivers Press • Thorndike Press
Bath, England • Thorndike, Maine USA

This Large Print edition is published by Chivers Press, England and by Thorndike Press, USA.

Published in 1998 in the U.K. by arrangement with HarperCollins Publishers.

Published in 1998 in the U.S. by arrangement with St. Martin's Press, Inc.

U.K. Hardcover ISBN 0–7540–3251–5 (Chivers Large Print)
U.K. Softcover   ISBN 0–7540–3252–3 (Camden Large Print)
U.S. Softcover   ISBN 0–7862–1381–7 (General Series Edition)

83039

MORAY COUNCIL

Department of Technical

& Leisure Services

F

Set in 16 pt. New Times Roman.

Printed in Great Britain on acid-free paper.

British Library Cataloguing in Publication Data available

Library of Congress Cataloging-in-Publication Data

Jeffries, Roderic, 1926-
    A maze of murders : an Inspector Alvarez novel / Roderic Jeffries.
    p. (alk. paper) cm.
    ISBN 0-7862-1381-7 (lg. print : sc : alk. paper)
    1. Large type books. I. Title.
    [PR6060.E43M39 1998]
    823'.914—dc21   97-52116

CHAPTER ONE

As life filtered back, it seemed to Sheard that someone had not only split open his head, but had also emptied some of the riper contents of a dustbin into his mouth. He opened his eyes to find himself staring at a curving ceiling which was so close that he thought it was descending to crush him. He whimpered as he struggled to move from wherever he was to wherever he could get to; his head struck something yielding. Despite the additional agony this promoted, he tilted his head up until he could see what he had touched. A pair of feet.

After a while, he managed to lift himself up on to one elbow. The feet belonged to a young woman who wore a pair of lime-green pants and occupied less than half the settee. Because she was on her back, he could see the mole just below her left breast. The mole seemed about to prompt a memory, but his confusion proved to be too great.

He looked to his right. Lying on the floor was a second young woman; she wore nothing. He could no longer support himself and collapsed. It might look like heaven, but it felt like hell. He closed his eyes and fell asleep. He regained consciousness and, despite the continuing agony in his head and vile taste in his mouth, became aware of an unusual warmth about his legs. He propped himself up, looked down at his naked body; from the middle of his thighs downwards, he was in sharp sunshine. He visually followed the shaft of light through a doorway and saw rails, a flagstaff, and brilliant blue sky.

The flagstaff unlocked his memory.

Lewis had been the first to spot Kirsty and Cara. They had been strolling along the pedestrianized front when they saw the girls watching a human statue. Lewis had started talking to them and after a short while, correctly judging Cara's off-hand manner to be no more than the initial declaration of I'm-not-the-sort-of-girl-you-seem-to-take-me-for, had suggested they move to one of the cafés for a drink.

Kirsty had been friendly, Cara had maintained an air of boredom until Lewis had suggested that they have one more drink then take a trip across the bay in his motor cruiser. Cara had jeeringly called him a liar who didn't have so much as a rowing boat, but had accompanied them along the eastern jetty and when Lewis had identified the *Aventura* as his, she had been the first to board.

They'd cast off and with Lewis at the helm had made their way out of harbour and into the bay. They'd sailed around for a while—getting to know each other—and had then anchored off the Hotel Parelona. In the saloon, Lewis had opened a cupboard and brought out two

2

bottles of whisky—one nearly empty, the other full—four glasses, and a pack of cigarettes. Cara had cast off any suggestion of boredom and the evening had proceeded along accepted lines. Initial refusal, token resistance, much giggling. But then things had not gone according to plan . . .

Sheard suddenly knew he was going to be very ill. He slithered off the settee too quickly and had to grab for support. As his stomach looped the loop, he realized he'd no idea where the heads were. Necessity also being the mother of improvisation, he staggered out of the saloon on to the deck and leaned over the rails to be far sicker than he had thought possible. It was a while before he overcame his misery sufficiently to notice the anchored yacht a hundred metres across the glinting sea on which two men and one woman were laughing. He remembered he was naked.

As he returned to the saloon and slumped down on the end of the settee, Cara began to move, then sat up. She stared at him, eyes bloodshot, expression drawn, looking older than she claimed to be. 'God, I feel awful! '

'No worse than I do.'

'How the bloody hell d'you know?' She moved a hand to her stomach and was surprised to discover she was naked. 'I'm going to be sick. Where's the loo?'

'I don't know.'

She struggled to her feet, lost her balance

3

and grabbed hold of Kirsty's hip for support. Kirsty made a sound that was midway between a grunt and a cry. Cara made for the for'd doorway.

He lay back and closed his eyes.

Cara returned. 'The loo's up the corridor but I can't get the bloody thing to work. It's all handles and wheels. What do I do?'

He shrugged his shoulders.

'I've known dead dogs more useful than you.' She slowly searched through the clothes that littered the deck and found hers. She pulled on panties, T-shirt, and skin-tight jeans. 'I feel I'm being choked.' She stumbled out on deck, grabbed the rails, and breathed heavily.

'What's happening?'

Kirsty's voice so startled him that he turned sharply; pain surged through his head. 'She needed more air.'

'It wouldn't do you any harm from the look of you. I said not to drink so much.'

'I didn't,' he muttered.

'If it wasn't the booze made it impossible, what was it?'

'What was what?'

She giggled.

Only a feeling of intense lethargy prevented his telling her how stupid her giggling sounded.

Cara returned to the saloon, tottered over to the starboard settee and collapsed on to it. 'I swear to God, not another drop if I live to be a hundred and fifty.'

'I told you, you were all drinking too much,' Kirsty said sanctimoniously.

'You would, wouldn't you?'

'I suppose Neil's even worse than you two?'

'I bloody hope so.'

'Where is he?'

'Who cares?'

'We'd better find him so he can take us back.'

'You find him if you're in such a hurry.'

Kirsty climbed off the settee, picked up her clothes from the deck and got dressed. She went for'd, soon to return. 'He's not inside so he must be outside.'

They said nothing.

She went aft and out on deck and they could hear her climb up to the flying bridge. When she came back, she said, worry edging her voice, 'He's not anywhere.'

Sheard opened his eyes. 'He's got to be.'

'Then you find him.' She came up to the settee. 'Move.'

'Why?'

She grabbed him and pulled. Cursing, he put his feet to the deck and stood. The effort threatened to bring fresh disaster, but by repeatedly swallowing heavily, he was able to persuade his stomach not to revolt a second time. He dressed.

He checked the wheelhouse, heads, for'd locker and flying bridge. Back in the saloon, he said: 'You're right.' He sat.

5

'Then what's happened to him?'

'Stop getting so excited,' Cara snapped. 'He's gone ashore.'

'Why?'

'Because he wanted to.'

'How'd he get there?'

'If he's half as smart as he thinks he is, he walked.'

'Skinny and with all the people from the ritzy hotel and on the other boats watching?'

'He'd love it . . . Anyways, how d'you know he was starkers?'

'His clothes are still on the floor.' She pointed.

Lying about the deck were a shirt, pants, jeans and sandals.

'He can't have gone ashore without his clothes,' Kirsty said.

'If he ain't on the boat, he must have done.'

'Why would he do a thing like that?'

'How would I know? Jeeze, you're making my head ten times worse. Can't you shut up?'

'Suppose he fell overboard? This could be terribly serious. Don't you understand?'

'Yes. You're being a bloody pain.'

'If he's missing, we've got to tell someone.'

'I'm not stopping you.'

Kirsty turned to face Sheard. 'Get us back.'

'Look, if we . . .'

'Move,' she shouted.

Anything for a quiet life. He stood and wished he had not.

CHAPTER TWO

The hotel was one of the few in the port still family-run; the staff were both pleasant and helpful. 'His key is on the board,' the receptionist said, in heavily accented English. 'He is not in his room.'

'Would you know if he returned during the night?' Kirsty asked.

He shook his head. 'For that, you must speak to the night person.'

'How can we?'

'He will be here at seven tonight.'

'That's no use.' Worry made her sound angry. 'We've got to talk to whoever was on the desk last night.'

'He sleeps. Perhaps after three in the afternoon . . .'

'Now!'

'Señorita, when a man has worked all the night . . .'

'Something terrible could have happened to Neil. We must know if he came back here during the night and is safe.'

'This is different. I phone Miguel and say why I wake him. One moment, please.' The receptionist reached across to the nearer telephone, lifted the receiver, dialled. When the connection was made, he spoke, listened,

7

spoke more rapidly, gesturing with his free hand. He looked up. 'His wife wakes him. She did not wish, but I explain, is necessary.'

They waited. When the receptionist began to speak over the phone again, Kirsty said: 'What's he saying?'

'I don't know,' Sheard answered.

'I thought you spoke Spanish?'

'He's talking Mallorquin.'

'Oh, God! I hope Neil did come back here.'

He agreed, his hope based on a different reason from hers. Since living in the port, he'd taken every possible care to keep as clear of the authorities as possible; if Lewis really were missing, he was going to have to bring himself to their attention.

The receptionist replaced the receiver. 'Miguel says señor not return. He knows for sure. The señor's room is fifteen and Miguel would have taken the number in the lottery if the señor want the key.'

'Perhaps . . .'

The two men looked at her and waited.

'He could just have returned, not gone to his room, and had breakfast.'

If Lewis had been suffering even half as badly as he was, Sheard thought, breakfast would have been off.

'Could you ask someone if he was here for breakfast?' she said.

The receptionist used the second telephone to speak to another member of staff. When the

8

brief call was over, he said: 'The waiter comes. Now, please excuse me.' He moved down the counter to speak to a woman.

They waited. A waiter, in the hotel's 'uniform' of open-neck white shirt, black trousers, and red cummerbund, came up to the desk and, at an indication from the receptionist, along to where they stood. 'You wish?' he asked, speaking English with great difficulty.

Sheard answered him in Spanish. He shook his head. 'The señor did not eat breakfast today. Of that, I can be certain.'

Sheard thanked him and he left. Even though it had been obvious what his answer had been, Kirsty said urgently: 'Well?'

'He didn't have breakfast.'

'Oh, God! . . . Then maybe he went to that hotel on the other side of the bay and is playing a joke on us. That's possible, isn't it?'

He was vaguely surprised that after the very brief acquaintance, she should become so emotionally concerned that she would clutch at non-existent straws. 'That's not the kind of hotel where you turn up dressed real casual. And since his clothes were still on the boat . . .'

'You've got to find out. You must phone and ask.'

'I don't think . . .'

'It doesn't matter what you think. Where's a phone we can use?'

'We'd best find a public one.'

'Then hurry instead of just standing around.'

As he followed her out of the hotel, the contrast between the cool interior and the heat and blinding light outside exacerbated his headache. He came to a stop.

'What is it?'

'My head's bursting.'

'Can't you forget that? Which way?'

'Turn right,' he muttered resentfully. He followed her along the broad pedestrian way, once a road, which, lined with palms, fronted by sand and sea, and sprinkled with tables protected by multicoloured sun umbrellas at which people ate and drank, epitomized the Mediterranean for most tourists.

They reached two public phones, back to back. He lifted the receiver of the one facing the direction in which they'd come, inserted a coin, dialled. No connection was made, but the coin disappeared into the interior of the machine instead of falling down for him to retrieve. He lacked the energy to swear. He moved round to the second phone and this time was more successful. The woman to whom he spoke said that no Señor Lewis had booked in at the hotel and she had no knowledge of anyone by that name.

As he replaced the receiver, Kirsty, her voice strained, said: 'What do we do now?'

'I don't know.'

'You've got to. You live here.'

'Sure. Only . . .' He lapsed into silence.

'We must tell the police.'
'Perhaps we should wait a bit longer . . .'
'Where's the police station?'
'A couple of roads back.'
'Then for God's sake, get moving.'
He led the way past numerous small shops, all catering to the tourist trade, to a building which only recently had become the office of the port's Policia Local—as the force was now called. In the front office, an overweight policeman with a Zapata moustache was reading a newspaper. He looked up, resumed reading.
'Kick some life into him,' she said.
'He'll react when he's ready. This is Spain.'
'And I'm English. Hey, Rip Van Winkle!'
The policeman finally put the paper down and stared at them with evident dislike.
'Good morning,' Sheard said in Spanish and in soapy tones. 'I trust we don't disturb you?'
'What's the matter?'
'We're very worried. A friend of ours may be missing and . . .'
'What do you mean, he may be? Either he is missing or he isn't.'
'We can't be certain.'
'Then come back when you can.'
'What's he saying?' she asked.
Sheard told her.
She faced the policeman and said angrily: 'It's your job to find out if anything has happened to him. So do something.'

The policeman had understood the import of her words, if not the words themselves. He brushed his moustache with crooked forefinger, picked up a pencil; the lead was broken and he put it down. He searched for and eventually found a ballpoint pen; it refused to work. He threw it into the wastepaper basket while expressing his opinion of the mothers of pen makers. He puffed as he hauled himself to his feet and left the room. When he returned, he had another ballpoint pen. He sat, opened a drawer of the desk and found it was empty, slammed it shut; in turn, he checked the other drawers without success. He left the room again, to return with a sheet of paper. He sat. 'Well? I haven't all day to waste.'

Sheard said: 'The four of us went by boat across the bay last night and had a bit of a party . . .'

'Where's your residencia?'

'I'm not a resident.'

'Where's your passport?'

'Back in my room.'

'Get it. And tell her to bring hers.' He pointed the pen at her, then slapped it down on the desk. He picked up the newspaper and, with evident satisfaction, resumed reading.

'Now what's up?' she asked in exasperation.

'We have to get our passports,' Sheard replied.

'What the hell for? What about Neil?'

'He won't listen until he's seen our

12

passports.'

'Then he needs kicking where it hurts.'

'Come on,' he said hurriedly. 'Let's go and get them.'

They had reached the doorway when the policeman said: 'Hombre, find yourself a Spanish girlfriend. She'll have better manners.'

CHAPTER THREE

Alvarez awoke. He stared up at the ceiling and knew a deep inner contentment. Life wore a golden hue. The previous day, a distant and almost forgotten relation of Jaime had visited them. Not only had he brought with him four bottles of Vega Sicilia, he had praised the lunch as one of the best meals he'd ever enjoyed. After he'd left, Dolores had declared him to be handsome, intelligent, and a man of cultured tastes. As always, her moods had been reflected in her cooking. Supper that evening had been a veritable feast.

Might a spirit of such beatitude continue? Could today's lunch be Pollastre farcit amb magrana? Even a cook of moderate ability would make something special of this dish of chicken, pork, lamb, pomegranate, wine, and seasoning; she could turn it into Lucullan fare . . .

She called up from downstairs that it was a

13

quarter past. He acknowledged that fact. After a while, he sat up, swivelled round on the bed, and put his feet on the floor, welcoming the coolness of the tiles. Already, the day was hot. Soon, it would be very hot. Heat was not conducive to work . . .

'It's half past. You'll be very late.'

Late was a word that was subject to many interpretations. By his, he was almost never late for work. He hauled himself to his feet and went along to the bathroom. Ten minutes later, he entered the kitchen and sat at the table.

'I've made some coca for you,' she said. 'I didn't start your chocolate until I heard you moving, but it's nearly ready.'

'There's no rush. There's very little work in hand and the superior chief is at a conference somewhere so he won't be making a nuisance of himself for a while.'

'Why is he always so difficult?'

'He comes from Madrid.'

'I had forgotten.' She was an elegant woman with a presence that could become commanding; with her jet-black hair, dark brown eyes, strong features, and upright carriage, it seemed apposite to picture her with mantilla and gold inlaid tortoiseshell comb, side-saddle on a caparisoned horse almost as proud as she. In fact, she had not a trace of Andaluce blood in her. She stirred the heating chocolate with a wooden spoon.

'I saw Diego last night,' he said. 'Asked to be

14

remembered to you.'

'The blackguard!'

'I thought you had a soft spot for him?'

'Doesn't stop him being a blackguard.'

'What's he done to deserve that?'

'Eulalia was so certain he would marry her that she crocheted a matrimonial bedspread, yet never once did he say or do anything that would allow her or her parents to demand he marry her. Then when Rosa appeared with many millions of pesetas—if one were evil-minded, one might ask how she earned them while she lived in Barcelona—he was after her as hard as he could run.'

'He was always a realist.'

'Only a man could say such a heartless thing!' Yet she spoke regretfully and not, as would have been normal, aggressively. 'Eulalia's heart was broken and her trousseau, on which she'd worked since she could first hold a needle, for her became rags.'

'Surely they came in handy when she married Narciso?'

'You can believe it was the same thing?'

He could, but clearly she couldn't.

She took the pan off the cooker, poured chocolate into a mug; she placed the mug, coca, and some membrilla on the table. 'I hope the coca's all right?'

It was very unusual for her to be diffident about the quality of her cooking. He cut a slice, spread membrilla on it, ate.

15

'Well?'

'There's not a pasteleria between here and La Coruna could equal it.'

She was satisfied. 'I must go and do the shopping for lunch.'

'Pollastre farcit amb magrana?'

She shook her head.

His disappointment was brief. Lunch would still be a feast.

She picked up a shopping bag and her purse, and left. He finished the coca on his plate and reached out to cut another slice, checked himself. Recently, the doctor had told him to smoke, drink, and eat less if he wanted many more birthdays. In the face of so stern a warning, he had sworn to take the advice to heart. But this coca was as light as a thrush's breast feather; and doctors always exaggerated in order to increase their self-importance.

He had just finished both coca and rich chocolate when the phone rang. He left the kitchen, went through the sitting/dining-room and into the front room.

'It's the Policia Local down in the port. Is that Inspector Alvarez?'

'Speaking.'

'It's about time! Talk about being one hell of a job to get hold of you—the post said you'd be at work at eight-thirty, but I've rung your office every quarter of an hour since then, trying to get hold of you. Finally, they gave me your home number.'

16

'I was called out unexpectedly and have only just returned for my breakfast.'

'There's a spot of trouble here. A couple of English came in yesterday to report a friend was missing from a boat and they didn't know what had happened to him; they've been in again this morning to say he still hasn't turned up.'

'Missing people are the Guardia's job.'

'But they say this isn't their pigeon until it's certain the man is missing and it's up to you to ascertain that.'

'They are a bunch of lazy bastards.'

'Who'll argue?'

'Why aren't they certain?'

'There's no body.'

'Of course there isn't since it'll take time to float to the surface.'

'Argue it out with them. I'm just the messenger. Señor Sheard, Señor Lewis, Señorita Fenn, and Señorita Glass sailed out from the port late on Thursday evening. They crossed the bay and anchored off the Hotel Parelona, had a drink, fell asleep. When they woke up, Señor Lewis wasn't aboard and there's been no sign of him since.'

*   *   *

The row of single-storey terrace houses along Carer Joan Sitjar (until recently, Calle General Ortega) had originally been fishermen's

17

cottages, offering only minimum shelter; however, each had had a garden at the back where vegetables and fruit could be grown, pigs and chickens kept. The rising tide of prosperity, fuelled by the tourist trade, had ensured that now they were in good repair and modernized to offer a considerable degree of comfort, but, since progress was always double-edged, owners were now forbidden to keep pigs or chickens in the gardens.

Alvarez braked to a halt in front of No. 14, whose walls were painted a light pink and doors and shutters green. He brought a handkerchief from his trouser pocket and mopped his face; the day was burning hot. He left the car, crossed the pavement, stepped through the bead curtain into the immaculately maintained front room. He called out.

A middle-aged woman, wearing an apron, hurried through the inner doorway. She studied him. 'Enrique!'

He knew her face but couldn't place her name.

'I saw Dolores only last week, up in the village where I go to buy vegetables because they're so much better than here where people only bother about selling to the foreigners. She said that . . .'

As he listened, he searched his memory and finally remembered who she was. When she paused, he said: 'How's Joaquin?'

There was another flood of words. Her

husband had had the bad fall when building a house for a German. What a house! More than forty million pesetas! Her father had bought his house for six hundred! Joaquin was much better and would be back to work very soon. She would be glad when he was. To have a man around the house all the time could drive a woman crazy. It was lucky they'd let the room to the Englishman—with no children of their own, because God had not been generous, they had an extra bedroom and it was stupid not to have someone sleeping in it who was willing to pay good pesetas. The Englishman played chess and for some of the time he kept Joaquin out of her way . . .

'The reason I'm here is to have a word with Señor Sheard.'

Sweet Mary, but one could never be certain when one arose in the morning that one would be alive to go to bed in the evening. To think that only a few days before, the Englishman had been sleeping in her house and now he was dead . . .

'But surely Señor Sheard is still alive?'

'What a question! Did I not give him breakfast before he left early this morning?'

'Then why did you say he was dead?'

'Didn't Dolores say to me, no man ever listens? Perhaps a fortnight ago, Bert came to me . . .'

'Who's Bert?'

'Who do you think? Señor Sheard.

Foreigners have Christian names, even if they sound so ugly that no saint would have them.' She spoke more quickly, raising her voice as one did when talking to someone slightly slow-witted. Bert met a friend who'd nowhere to stay and had asked if he might share the room. Naturally, she'd been about to refuse—some things happened in the world that a decent woman did not wish to know about—when Bert had added that his friend would naturally pay the same rent as he did. Whatever one thought about such things, only a complete fool spat on a peseta. So she'd said yes. Regretfully, after a few days the friend had left to stay at the Hotel Vista Bella. Now he was dead! Aiee, life was but death delayed!

'We don't yet know he is dead.'

'Four people go to sleep in a boat in the bay and in the morning there are only three. You think he sprouted wings and flew?'

He thought that women made lousy detectives.

CHAPTER FOUR

The Hotel Alhambra, one road back from the front, catered for the lower range package holiday trade; rooms were small, the en-suite shower rooms a tight fit for one person, meals were poor and served buffet-style, and the staff were less than willing because guests seemed to think that a hundred-peseta tip was generous.

Alvarez walked around a mound of luggage belonging to a departing group of guests and up to the reception desk, manned by a young man. 'Are Señoritas Fenn and Glass in the hotel?'

'How would I know?' replied the receptionist, his attention on a young woman in a bikini who was crossing the foyer to go out to the beach.

'By checking.'

'Too busy.'

'Cuerpo General de Policia.'

He reluctantly looked at the register, then up at the key board. 'Their key's not there, so they'll be around somewhere.'

'Then ask someone to find out where.'

The receptionist muttered sullenly to himself, opened a door to the rear of the counter, and shouted. A teenager appeared and was given the order.

'Is there a lounge where I can have a word with them?' Alvarez asked.

The receptionist pointed.

He walked across the foyer and into a small room, depressingly decorated and furnished. If the declared aim of upgrading all hotels on the island was ever actually implemented, he thought, this one was a prime candidate for immediate attention. He sat on a shabby settee and waited with the endless patience of a

21

peasant.

A woman entered and looked uncertainly at him. 'I am Inspector Alvarez,' he said. She was hardly a model of discretion; her hair was too blonde, her make-up too generous, her dress too tight-fitting. 'You are Señorita Glass or Señorita Fenn?'

'Cara. I mean, Cara Fenn. Kirsty's gone with Bert to speak to the police again. I couldn't go because . . . because it's all too emotional.'

Couldn't be bothered, he thought uncharitably. He waited until she was seated, then said: 'I have to ask you some questions, but will be as brief as possible.'

'Then you haven't found Neil?'

'I fear not.'

'He . . . he's dead?'

'There still can be no certainty and that is why I am here now.'

'But I don't know where he is.'

'Of course not, but you may be able to help me ascertain where he might be if still alive . . . Have you known the señor for a long time?'

She shook her head.

'When did you first meet him?'

'That night.'

'You mean, Thursday?'

'Yes.'

'Please tell me how you met him.'

She and Kirsty had had supper—like always, funny tasting and not what they were used to at home—and had then left the hotel to go to the

22

front. They'd strolled along until they'd stopped to watch a woman in a long white dress and with whitened face and gloved hands who had been imitating a statue and moving only when someone put money in the collecting box. Neil had set out to make the woman laugh and had drawn them into his attempt; he'd suggested drinks at one of the bars; after a while, he'd said it was such a lovely night they ought to go for a trip in his boat . . .

'The boat belonged to him?'

'Seemed like it did. I mean, he had the key to unlock the cabin and start the engine.'

'You sailed across the bay?'

She nodded. Then she said: 'If only we'd stayed. Then it wouldn't have happened. I can't stop thinking that if only I'd said I didn't want to go, he'd be alive.'

He was satisfied she spoke only for effect. 'Señorita, sadly one can never move back in time and it only makes things more painful to try and do so. What happened once you'd anchored?'

'We had a drink.'

'You'd taken this with you?'

'There were a couple of bottles of whisky on the boat.'

'Were they full bottles?'

'One of 'em was, the other didn't have much in it.'

'Did you finish them both?'

'Give over.'

23

'Then how much did you all drink?'

'Hardly had any out of the full bottle . . . Look, I'm not a lush.'

'Of course not, señorita, but I need to understand what state you and your companions were in because that could be very important.'

'I was cheerful, nothing more.'

'And Señor Lewis?'

'We was all the same.'

'Did you do anything other than drink?'

'What's that matter?'

'As I explained, I need to understand all the circumstances which surround the señor's disappearance.'

She said nothing.

'Señorita, you must tell me.'

'I . . . We . . . You know how it goes.'

'Not until you tell me.'

'We started to have some fun,' she said reluctantly.

'You mean, you had sexual intercourse?'

'There's no call to be crude . . . A girl's entitled to a little fun.'

'With one señor, or both?'

'For God's sake, what d'you take me for?'

He was tempted to answer, but didn't.

'If you must know, nothing happened.'

'Why was that?'

'Because it didn't.'

'The señor had drunk too much?'

'If he'd been that tight, I wouldn't have had

24

anything to do with him. I can't stand drunks.'

'Yet if he wasn't . . . Why did nothing happen?'

'Because we both fell asleep,' she said angrily, certain he must be laughing at her.

Surprise, not contemptuous amusement, was his reaction. It seemed the English did not live up to their reputation. 'Señorita, I have to tell you that what you've said suggests the señor had drunk very much more than you wish to admit.'

'I'm not a liar.'

'But it is very difficult to believe that if sober, he would have fallen asleep at such a moment.'

'I don't care how difficult, that's how it went.'

'Was Señor Lewis a good swimmer?'

'He said he was. Talked about winning medals when he was younger, but like as not that was flannel to try to impress us.'

'When you and your friends awoke in the morning, you found his clothes were still aboard?'

'Yeah.'

'Did he have a bathing costume with him?'

'I never saw one.'

He was about to speak again when a young woman looked into the lounge, saw Cara, stepped inside. 'Everything all right?' she asked.

'No, it bloody well isn't,' Cara answered.

'What's wrong?'

25

'He's trying to call me a liar.'

The answer confused her.

'Are you Señorita Glass?' Alvarez asked.

She nodded.

Whenever two women went around together, it always seemed that one was more obviously attractive than the other. Even a Frenchman would not have described Kirsty as more than pleasant looking. 'I am Inspector Alvarez.'

Kirsty said: 'We've just been to see the police again and they don't know anything. Do you?'

'I very much regret not, señorita. Which is why I am here to try and discover what might have happened to the señor.'

'By asking bloody rude questions,' Cara said resentfully.

He turned. 'I am sorry, señorita, if I have disturbed you, but there are times when a detective has to be rather like a doctor . . .'

'And most of them are dirty old men!'

Kirsty looked worried, afraid that Alvarez would take sharp offence.

He said quietly: 'Señorita Glass, please come and sit down so that I can discover if you can help me.'

As Kirsty moved forward, Cara said: 'I've told you all I know, so there's no point in me staying.'

'That is so. But first, how much longer are you staying here?'

'A week.' She hesitated, but when nothing

26

more was said, she stood and left, hips swinging.

He spoke to Kirsty: 'Tell me as much as you can remember of Thursday night.'

Her description of the evening was considerably more detailed than Cara's had been and she showed no embarrassment when describing the more intimate moments.

Her manner reminded him of the old saying, The fastest running torrente is not always the deepest. 'Señorita, am I correct to believe you did not drink as much as the others?'

'I've a bit of a funny tummy and it's very easily upset, so I have to be careful.'

'Yet perhaps you had drunk rather more than you think since you were ill on Friday morning?'

'Not half as ill as the other two. And I do remember exactly how much I had.'

'Then you must be surprised that you were so affected?'

'In a way, I suppose so. But maybe booze is just grabbing me more than it used to.'

'Are you certain that the first bottle of whisky was emptied before the second one was opened?'

'Yes. Wouldn't you expect it to be?'

He nodded. 'Was Señor Lewis drunk by the time he opened the second one?'

'No way. He was full of himself, suggesting all sorts of things, but that seemed to be his style.'

'His speech wasn't slurred or his movements uncoordinated?'

'If you ask me, at that stage they were very coordinated.' She began to giggle, then stopped abruptly. 'I shouldn't say things like that, should I, in case he is dead?'

'Señorita, it seems very likely he would prefer to be remembered with a laugh . . . Was Señor Sheard drunk?'

'He was like Neil, still talking normal and all that sort of thing. Only he wasn't able to . . .'

Alvarez waited. Finally, he said; 'Tell me again what happened after Señor Lewis opened the second bottle.'

For a moment it seemed she might question the need for the repetition, then she spoke quickly and, as before, without any trace of embarrassment. Sheard had drunk his whisky quickly, she'd sipped hers. Cara and Lewis, on the starboard settee, had started to explore each other's attractions and so they'd done the same. Sheard had yawned as he'd fondled her and become annoyed when she'd laughed. Then, as he took off his trousers and pants, he'd suddenly complained of dizziness; that was when she'd also first felt a bit dizzy. He'd tried to show further interest in her, but failed. To her surprise, and it had to be admitted annoyance, he'd fallen asleep. She'd looked across the cabin to see if the other two were laughing at her, but they were both asleep. Then she'd felt overwhelmingly tired and she'd

28

fallen asleep.

'The last drink was from the second bottle?'

'That's right.'

'And Señor Lewis opened it. Will you describe how he opened it?'

'What d'you mean? There's only one way, isn't there?'

'If it was a full bottle, the cap should have been sealed. Did he have to exert force to break the seal?'

'He must have done.'

'What I'm asking,' he said patiently, 'is whether you can recall his having to use such force? The cap can be sealed so firmly that it's quite a struggle to free it.'

'I see what you mean . . . As I remember, he just unscrewed. What's it matter?'

'I'm not sure that it does,' he answered casually. 'Presumably, Señor Lewis poured out a drink for himself as well as for the rest of you?'

'He's not the one to forget himself.'

He was silent for a few seconds, then said: 'You woke up yesterday morning, discovered the señor was missing and decided to return to the port to find out if he had been playing a silly joke; if not, to report his disappearance. Do you by any chance remember what happened to the second bottle of whisky?'

'Not really.'

'I have just one more question. From the moment you fell asleep on the boat to the time

29

when you woke up, can you remember anything at all?'

'No.' She began to fiddle with the hem of her T-shirt. 'That is . . .'

He said nothing.

'It sounds so silly.'

'I assure you I will not find it so.'

'It's just . . . I seem to remember thinking I could hear someone moving around. I don't know why, but this had me so scared that I was desperate to escape, only I couldn't move and it was as if I'd been paralysed. Then the sounds stopped and things went all black again. When I told Cara about this, she said it was a stupid nightmare. I suppose it must have been. Only I can't stop wondering . . .' She paused, then spoke in a rush. 'Wondering that maybe it was Neil I'd heard and if only I'd managed to wake up properly I could have tried to save him if he did fall over the side. But it was like I was in a dense fog . . .' She became silent, her expression strained.

'Señorita, it is most likely that your friend is right and it was a nightmare.'

But a waking nightmare?

CHAPTER FIVE

The sign prohibited a left turn. Alvarez swore. Every time he drove around the port, the road system seemed to have been altered; planning was clearly in the hands of someone with an interest in the manufacture of road signs. He took the next left turn, then could find nowhere to park. He swore at greater length. Ten years before, this area had been fields over which birds had flown, now it was all concrete. When people lauded the benefits that tourism brought, did they also list the spiritual values that it took? ... A car drew out, leaving a parking space and as he drew into this his mood immediately lightened.

He walked the short distance to the police station and went inside. The duty officer was an old acquaintance and so they chatted for several minutes before he said: 'I need to talk to someone at the Institute of Forensic Anatomy; all right if I use your phone?'

'Sure.'

He reached across for the phone on the desk, lifted the receiver, dialled. When the connection was made, he asked to speak to Professor Fortunato or one of his assistants.

A man said: 'Luis Jodar here.'

'I need to know what happens when someone drowns at sea.'

'He dies.'

Every man a comic! 'But does the body float or sink; if it sinks, does it later return to the surface?'

'I'll give you the answers, but you must remember, they're generalizations. There's

31

always some awkward bastard who'll make nonsense of the standard figures.'

Bureaucrats were forever covering themselves.

'When a person falls into the water he swims, if he can, until he's too exhausted to continue; if he can't, he starts to panic immediately. Panicking means he ingests water into the air passages which increases the panic and the water begins to collect in his lungs to mix with the air and the mucus to form a choking froth. The weight of water gradually causes first neutral buoyancy, then negative, and at some point the victim makes one last convulsive threshing movement and then dies. Because of the negative buoyancy, the body remains below the surface. After a time, gasses begin to form and these increase buoyancy until it becomes positive and the body surfaces. This normally takes between five and eight days, but in really warm weather the time can be halved. You'll want to know about the signs of putrefaction . . .'

'No, thanks,' Alvarez said hurriedly.

'They can be very interesting. And by the way, that old story that as one drowns, one sees the whole of one's past life—don't panic, you may die in bed.'

As he thanked the other, Alvarez reflected that a macabre job promoted a macabre sense of humour.

He left the police station and drove to the

eastern arm of the harbour where he parked. He stepped out into the harsh sunshine and considered the yachts and motor cruisers immediately in front of him, those at more distant berths which were marked by masts or superstructures, and those which he couldn't see at all from where he stood, and wondered how many billions of pesetas were moored about him; billions of pesetas whose only purpose was to massage men's egos. If only all that money were used on the land to produce better crops . . . A fool cried to the moon for help. Burgeoning prosperity had turned men's priorities inside out; luxuries had become more prized than essentials.

The harbour-master's office was in a building which dated back to the time when the harbour had been very small and used only by fishermen—there was storage and drying space available for the few who still fished commercially. Alvarez entered the office and Torres, past retiring age but not yet retired, looked up. 'Enrique!' He stood, came round his desk and shook hands. 'It's a long time; too long.' No taller than Alvarez, he was considerably more overweight. 'Grab that chair and sit and tell me how the family is.'

Twenty minutes later, Alvarez brought the conversation round to work. 'Not heard any more about the Englishman who's missing from a boat, I suppose?'

'I'd have been in touch if the body had

turned up. It's early days. Remember Manuel Coix?'

'Can't say I do.'

'Awkward, bad-tempered bastard, but a real fisherman. When I was a kid there was a bad time when the other boats came in with hardly enough fish even to feed the families of the crews, but he'd tie up with the gunwale all but awash because of his catch. There were some who claimed he'd sold his soul and the devil drove the fish into his nets and on to his hooks, but my dad laughed at that—why would the devil pay so much for his soul when it wasn't worth a single céntimo? No, Manuel was a seaman as well as a fisherman; he'd look up at the sky and study the clouds, feel the wind against his cheeks, note the way the water was moving, and he'd know where the fish were. Never shared the news, of course; if he ever gave as much as a crust of dried bread to a starving child, no one heard about it.' He half turned to look through the window. 'There's not a single seaman amongst the owners of the boats out there. Take away the radios, position-finders, radars, and navigation computers, and there's not one could steer a straight course from here to Menorca or splice a good dog's cock.'

'But even though Manuel was such a good seaman, he drowned?'

'Died in his bed, cursing his woman for a puta and his son for a spineless waster. What

34

are you on about?'

'From the way you were talking, I thought he must have drowned.'

'It was the youngster he took with him. There was talk he must be Manuel's by-blow otherwise he'd never have been taken into the boat, seeing he was so square-fisted he'd tangle a line as he picked it up. Anyway, this kid insisted on wearing thigh-length sea boots, so when he fell over the side—which, being so clumsy, was inevitable—he went straight down. There wasn't sight of him for a month until what remained of him was found by one of the boats . . . So it'll likely be a time before the Englishman turns up.'

'Palma says a body will float after five to eight days in normal water, half that time if it's really warm.'

'It'll be the sea what decides, not Palma.'

'Assuming he fell over the side and drowned . . .'

'What d'you mean, assuming?'

'It's still not certain what happened. Would you expect the body to be taken out to sea?'

'Sometimes there's a current, sometimes there ain't; sometimes it'll sweep things round and round the bay, sometimes it'll take 'em straight out to sea.'

'Would you know what the current's been doing since Thursday night?'

'Not so as I could pinpoint where it could've taken the body.'

'What's the name of the boat?'

'*Aventura*. Half the boats are called that. Give 'em an adventure at sea and they'd need to change their pants.'

'Who owns it?'

'Are you that ignorant? A boat's a she.'

'I've always wondered why.'

'Because you never know what the bitch is going to do next.'

'So who owns her?'

'Gomila y Hijos. The company's head office is in Barcelona so when it comes to the pesetas, they're as sharp as a skinning knife. They charter boats—they've two more here and several around the south coast.'

'Has the company got a local office?'

'Along the front, past the new restaurant that's opened.'

'What's their food like?'

'Good enough for the tourist who thinks a few bits of scrag chicken, a couple of rings of squid, and a small prawn make a paella.'

Alvarez spoke reflectively. 'Remember when Guillermo owned the Pescador and did the cooking? Even Dolores couldn't better his paella . . . That was on his good days, of course. When he and Inés had been rowing, you seldom knew what you'd be eating.'

'Or if you did, you didn't eat it.'

'One peseta; or was it one peseta fifty?'

'Two with a carafe of wine.'

'I often wondered where he found that

36

wine—never tasted anything like it before or since.'

'They said he went round all the bodegas, buying up the lees.'

'I'll believe that.'

'Still, for fifty céntimos you couldn't expect Marqués de Riscal.'

For a while they continued to reminisce, remembering the past in rosy colours and forgetting the harsh conditions, the uncertainties, the fears that had prevailed. Then Alvarez said goodbye and left. He returned to his car and drove along the front, past the new restaurant—already a number of tables were occupied; few tourists were selective—and stopped in a no-parking area. He walked back to the offices of Gomila y Hijos.

A young woman sat in front of a VDU and painted her nails. She looked up briefly, returned her attention to her nails.

'I wonder if you can help me,' Alvarez said.

'Doubt it.'

'I need to know who chartered the *Aventura*.'

'What's it to you?'

'Cuerpo General de Policia.'

'You don't look like you're anything to do with them.'

'It is the good Lord who decides our looks, not our jobs,' he said pompously. Nostalgia for the past increased. Twenty-five years ago, she would have treated him with considerable respect.

She studied the nail she had just painted. 'What is it, then?'

'Have you not heard that an Englishman who sailed on the *Aventura* on Thursday night is missing?'

'Oh, that,' she said dismissively.

Her indifference angered him. 'I want to know the name of the person who chartered the boat,' he said roughly.

She replaced the brush in the bottle, screwed down the cap, breathed on her nails to make certain the varnish had dried, finally turned to the computer. She tapped out instructions, studied the screen. 'He did.'

'Señor Lewis? Are you certain?'

'It's on screen, isn't it?'

'How long did he charter her for?'

'A fortnight.'

'What did it cost him?'

'A hundred and fifty thousand.'

He whistled.

'It's only a small cruiser. A decent sized one would've cost him double that,' she said disdainfully, contemptuous of his ignorance of life in the rich lane.

CHAPTER SIX

Alvarez was able to park immediately in front of No. 14. He crossed the pavement, stepped through the bead curtain, called out.

Christina came through to the front room. 'You again! How am I supposed to do a proper day's work when you keep interrupting me?'

'This will be the last time. Has Señor Sheard returned yet?'

'Came back half an hour ago.'

'Then I'll have a word with him.'

'You'll not be long. It's his meal soon and I'll not have that getting cold.'

He looked at his watch and was surprised to see that it was one o'clock. 'I'll be quick. Where will I find him?'

'This way.'

She led him through a sitting-room that was far from luxuriously furnished, but was immaculately clean and tidy, to a doorway that gave access to a small open patio. 'He's on the other side.'

In the patio, which was no more than four metres by three, there grew an orange and two tangerine trees, whose fruit was small and green, and on the south-facing dividing wall, an ancient vine whose many bunches of grapes were just beginning to darken. On the far side was an open space in which was a wash area with a sink hewn out of rock and a single room.

The door of the room was swung back and clipped to the wall. 'Señor Sheard,' he called out, before stepping through the bead curtain. Sheard, wearing only shorts, lay on the bed, reading, a noisy fan directed at his chest. 'My name is Inspector Alvarez.'

Sheard dropped the paperback and propped himself up on one elbow. 'Have you heard something?'

'I'm afraid not.'

'Then he . . . he must be dead?'

'We still cannot be certain, which is why I need to ask you a few questions.'

'Are you the bloke who's been talking to Kirsty and Cara?'

'I am.'

'I can't tell you anything more than them.'

'I'm sure you'll be able to help, even if only to confirm what they have said . . . May I sit?' He removed a pile of magazines from the seat of a chair, sat. 'I need to learn more about Señor Lewis. Does he live on the island?'

'It's his first visit here.'

'He came from England?'

'I can't rightly say.'

'He is not a great friend of yours?'

'I only met him a fortnight ago.'

'Tell me about that meeting.'

'There's nothing to tell.'

'All the same, describe it.'

'Well, I was just having a drink in one of the bars and talking to a bloke I know. When he left, Neil came up, having heard me speaking English. Wanted to know if I could help him. He'd arrived on the night ferry and needed a bed. He'd asked around the hotels and aparthotels, but the only one with a free room

40

was asking more than he could afford; he thought I might know somewhere he could kip down. I took him along to the hostal, but that was full and the one up in the village is being reformed so that wasn't any good. We went into another bar and had a few drinks and I got to thinking he seemed a nice enough bloke so I said that if the old woman who owns this place didn't object, he could doss down with me. She charged, of course. They'd screw the last penny out of their own sick grandmothers . . .' He stopped abruptly, realizing his words had become offensive.

Alvarez ignored the comment, certain Sheard was of too limited an intelligence to appreciate that if one had known a time when poverty was no more than a few céntimos away, one grabbed every possible peseta to make as certain as possible that such a time did not return. 'What caused the row between you?'

'Row? What row?'

'Señor Lewis left here and moved into the Hotel Vista Bella.'

'That wasn't because of any row. It was just that things were so cramped here and . . .'

'Yes?'

'It gave a better impression.'

'To whom?'

'The birds.' He looked quickly at Alvarez and saw he had not been understood. 'It helps to make friends with the women if it looks like you're flash.'

Scheming liar, Alvarez thought, conveniently forgetting the days of his youth when he'd changed into a newly ironed shirt and carefully pressed trousers before joining the paseo in the village square. 'If this is Señor Lewis's first trip to the island, does he have friends who live or who are staying here whom he visited?'

'He doesn't know anyone.'

He noted the vehemence with which Sheard had answered the question. People who lacked self-confidence often tried to mask a lie by sudden forcefulness. 'I expect you can tell me which local bank he's been using?'

'Not used one.'

'Are you sure? If he hasn't drawn a large sum of money through a bank and has no friends who have provided him with funds, how is it that when he first arrived he could not afford to stay at a good hotel, yet after a few days he not only moved into one, but also paid a large sum of money to charter a motor cruiser?'

Sheard, his expression now sullen, did not answer.

'You don't know how?'

'No.'

'The question hasn't intrigued you?'

'I mind my own business.'

Sheard's hands and body were tensed and beads of sweat were pricking his forehead despite the relative coolness of the room. Yet weakness could become strength through desperation. Alvarez decided that for the moment it was best not to pursue the matter directly any further but there might be another way to confirm that the other was lying. 'The two of you have been going around together?'

'Yes.'

'For much of the time?'

'All the time.'

'Then you do not have a job?'

'No.' Once again, he spoke with unnecessary force.

'Then you are a lucky man since you do not have to work to live! Your money comes from England?'

'Yes.'

'Which bank here handles the transfer?'

'What . . . Why d'you want to know?'

'In my job, I have to confirm as much as possible, whether or not it's really of any importance. So I will need to ask your bank to confirm what you've just said.'

Sheard began to fidget. 'I . . .' He flicked the edges of the paperback. He spoke in a rush. 'Friends bring the money out in travellers' cheques.'

'At which bank or banks have you changed these?'

There was no answer.

Alvarez's tone was friendly. 'Señor, do not forget that I am Mallorquin.'

'What's that supposed to mean?'

'Should I learn of a foreigner who has a job,

but who forgets to inform the authorities and in consequence does not pay any tax, my only response is envy. I feel no desire to denounce him.'

Sheard hesitated.

'Of course, if I discover that fact in the course of an investigation and there is no way of concealing it from my report, my superior, who is Spanish, may well be of a different mind.'

Sheard drew a deep breath. 'All right, I do odd jobs for the ex-pats.' He suddenly showed a rare flash of pride. 'There's always plenty of work going because they're either too old or too superior to do it themselves. And I'm good at the work.'

Since Sheard had been lying the second time he had spoken so forcefully, it seemed reasonable to assume that the first occasion had also masked a lie. But why lie about Lewis's knowing or visiting anyone? Because this had a direct bearing on the other's disappearance? Yet whilst it was easy to envisage Sheard's engaging in some minor criminal activity at no apparent risk to himself, it was difficult to believe he would do so if the crime were major and the physical risk obvious. But, of course, if his half-formulated interpretation of events was correct, there had been no physical risk. And the reward? Surely that had in some way to be connected with Lewis's new-found wealth? . . . 'Señor, please

44

tell me all you can remember about Thursday night, from the moment you met the two señoritas.'

Heartened by Alvarez's friendly manner and apparent dismissal of what had gone before, Sheard spoke with a measure of confidence. His evidence only twice contradicted Kirsty's and on each occasion the point was of no consequence.

'You have a good memory,' Alvarez said flatteringly. 'Perhaps it will help me clear up one final point. When Señor Lewis opened the second bottle of whisky, did it look as if he had to break the seal of the cap?'

'I wasn't watching. But seeing it was a full bottle, the top would've been sealed, wouldn't it?'

Alvarez was surprised that Sheard had not spoken forcefully.

*   *   *

Alvarez parked, crossed the pavement, and entered the front room. The air tingled with the scent of cooking. In the dining-room, Jaime sat at the table, a bottle of brandy and an empty glass in front of him. 'I don't know what's for grub, but it's making me hungry.'

Alvarez brought a glass out of the sideboard, filled the glass with brandy, added two cubes of ice from the insulated container. 'From the smell, it could be Estofat de xot. She's not

45

cooked that for months.'

'You're making me even hungrier!' Jaime reached across the table for the bottle, but as he did so there was the swish of the bead curtain to warn him that Dolores was coming through from the kitchen. He hastily withdrew his hand.

Face damp with sweat, she stepped into the dining-room. 'I'm sorry, but the meal's going to be a bit late because the shopping took such a long time, what with not finding what I wanted and meeting people who would talk.'

'She who travels slowly prolongs the pleasure of arriving,' Alvarez said.

'There's not much pleasure in shopping with all the foreigners around.' She turned. 'You've time for another drink,' she said over her shoulder as she went back into the kitchen.

Jaime picked up the bottle. 'Where did you learn these peculiar things you say?'

'Probably at school.'

'Bloody odd school you must have gone to.' He refilled his glass. He drank, put the glass down, looked at the bead curtain and said in a low voice: 'Have you noticed Dolores? '

'What about her?'

'I think something's up.'

Alvarez's concern was immediate. 'You mean, she's ill?'

'Not exactly ill. But acting strange. Comes in here a moment ago and says the meal's going to be late so have another coñac. You know what

46

she's usually like. Says I'm a drunkard when I'm on my first drink. Another thing. It's days since she's yelled at me over anything. Why's she like this?'

'How would I know? Maybe it's because your cousin made such a hit with her.'

'Are you suggesting she and him . . .?'

'Have you gone crazy? If she heard you suggest that, she'd yell so hard your brains would scramble.'

'Well it just seemed like that's what you were implying.'

'Do yourself a favour and stop thinking.'

'But it makes me worry, her behaving like this.'

'If a man offers you a lamb for free, don't bother to ask him where he got it.'

'I suppose you learned that at your school as well?' He drank deeply. 'Well, I'm glad I didn't go to it.'

CHAPTER SEVEN

Built before the Civil War, Hotel Vista Bella had catered for wealthy families from Palma or the Peninsula who spent much of the summer enjoying the quiet tranquillity of the port. Then, events both inside and outside Spain had dramatically affected the number of such guests and times had become very hard. The advent of the package holiday trade had offered a return to prosperity, but the family who owned the Vista Bella had been reluctant to accept it because they had had the foresight to realize that it must change the character of the hotel. Strangely, they had not at first realized that it must to an even greater degree change the whole character of the port with the result that the wealthy, whose prime requirement was exclusivity, would no longer favour it. Events, however, had soon forced them to acknowledge the fact that if they were to stay in business, they had to come to terms with the change. They had modernized and greatly enlarged the hotel, but in keeping with their ethos had—in so far as this was possible—continued to run it with the caring efficiency shown in the past, despite the fact that many of the guests bore little resemblance to their predecessors.

Alvarez turned off the pavement, went down the stone steps and into the foyer. He spoke to the desk clerk and explained that he wanted to examine Señor Lewis's room. The desk clerk called the assistant manager who, since the manager was not present and responsibility could not therefore be shifted, finally and reluctantly agreed to the request.

Room 24 had a wide balcony and Alvarez stepped on to this, stared out at the bay, and wondered if the many tourists ever appreciated to the full the beauty that lay before them. He sighed. Judging by the average tourist, it seemed unlikely.

He returned to the room. On the bedside table was a paperback with a lurid cover; the single drawer was empty. The dressing-table had nothing on it that was not hotel provided; the drawers were empty. He crossed to the built-in cupboard and slid back the right-hand door. On the floor was a battered canvas hold-all in which was dirty clothing, a pornographic video tape bought locally, and a carton of Lucky Strike which still contained four packs. By the side of the hold-all was a pair of brown shoes, in the left-hand one of which was a thick wad of banknotes. Mostly of ten thousand peseta denomination, they added up to seven hundred and sixteen thousand pesetas. He folded them up and replaced them. Hanging up were two pairs of jeans and a denim jacket. In the breast pocket of the jacket was a passport, a wallet which contained seven thousand pesetas, a five-pound note, and a packet of condoms; in other pockets were a crumpled up receipt from Gomila y Hijos, another, even more crumpled, from a restaurant in Bitges, and a used train ticket from Bitges to Barcelona.

He stood at the foot of the nearer bed and mentally reviewed the facts. Lewis had over seven hundred thousand pesetas in cash, yet only days previously he had been virtually penniless; the money and the passport surely negated the possibility—a very slight one—that his disappearance had been intended; prior to arriving on the island he had been on the Peninsula, yet had not told Sheard this (if Sheard were to be believed) . . .

He'd come to the hotel hoping to find answers; he seemed only to have raised more questions. He left and drove to the harbour, parked on the eastern arm and walked to where the *Aventura* was moored, dwarfed by the gin palace in the next berth. The gangplank was narrow and lacked any hand ropes, but most would have crossed it without a second thought. Altophobia provoked a hundred and one thoughts and caused him to have to summon up every ounce of willpower before he could make the crossing, miserably conscious of the ridiculous figure he cut.

The saloon door was shut, but not locked. He went inside and was gratified to see that nothing had been cleared up. On the port side, immediately for'd of the settee, was a table on which were three glasses, one of them on its side, an empty bottle of Bell's whisky and another over three-quarters full; on the deck by the starboard settee was a glass on its side, a T-shirt, jeans, pants, and a pair of sandals.

He picked up the two bottles and four glasses, put them in a plastic carrier bag retrieved from under the table. Once more, very frightened, he walked the plank.

He drove into the port and along to a dingy

50

bar in one of the backstreets owned by a man who, despite the fact he was illiterate, had a keen business brain and charged tourists in search of local colour twice as much as his regular customers.

'You look like you've just lost the winning lottery ticket,' the owner said, as he put a glass of brandy in front of Alvarez.

'That's just how I feel.'

'Woman trouble?'

'I've more important things to worry about.'

'If you think there's anything more important, you're getting really old.'

*   *   *

The bank's new branch in the village was laid out on the open plan, with the manager's desk in full view of customers but partitioned off by plate glass. Contrary to traditional caricature, the manager was cheerful and friendly and he actually enjoyed helping people overcome their financial problems, especially if while doing so he could enjoy the Mallorquin pastime of circumventing one or more of the multitude of rules and regulations. A short, rotund man, balding, yet with bushy eyebrows, he came round the desk and shook hands. 'Nice to see you, Enrique. How's the family?'

'They're all well,' Alvarez replied.

'Give Jaime and Dolores my regards... Now, how can I help you?'

'I need some information.'

'In connection with what?'

'On the face of things, there's been an accident and a man's drowned. Only there's no body so it's not certain he's dead; and if he is, I've the feeling it wasn't an accident. So if I can establish that there is a motive for his death, things should become clearer. Do you follow me?'

'I hope so.'

'I'll put it in concrete terms. A man arrives on the island and is hard put to rub two five-hundred-peseta coins together; yet within a few days he's staying at the Vista Bella, chartering a motor cruiser for a hundred and fifty thousand, and has well over seven hundred thousand in cash. It seems logical to suppose that the newly acquired wealth has a direct connection with his disappearance and I'm trying to find out if logic is fact.'

The manager rested his elbows on the desk, joined the tips of his fingers together. 'And the inference is?'

'Drug trade,' Alvarez replied succinctly. 'Killed because he was trying to pull a fast one on either the supplier or the purchaser. I might gain a lead if I can identify the source of the money.'

'So you're going to ask me to check for details of movements of unusually large amounts of cash?'

'And to ask all other banks to do the same.'

'But unfortunately you do not have a court order calling on us to co-operate?'

'It would take forever to get that. And in this case, time could be very important.'

The manager said reflectively: 'It's only a few days since I learned that the son of a cousin of mine has had to go into a clinic which deals with drug abuse . . . Can you suggest any names to make the search easier?'

'The best. I can offer is the reasonable certainty that the money will have been drawn by someone who speaks English.'

'Hardly much use when there are thousands of British residents on the island . . . This will take time.'

*　　　*　　　*

Despite having enjoyed a good siesta, Alvarez found it very difficult to stay wide awake as he sat in the stuffy office. Soon, it became impossible. He settled back in the chair, closed his eyes, and allowed his mind to wander. It had just attained the gentle incoherence which immediately preceded sleep when the telephone rang. After a while, it became silent. Contentedly, he recalled the comment of the Duke of Plesencia when informed that his wife had just died. Even a hurricane must cease. His mind once more drifted peacefully . . . The phone rang again.

Swearing, he wriggled into an upright

position, reached forward and picked up the receiver.

'Inspector Alvarez?'

There was, alas, no mistaking the plum-filled voice. 'Speaking, señorita.'

'I have been trying to ring you, but there has been no answer.'

'I have only just got back from some outside work.'

'The superior chief wishes to speak to you.'

'I thought he was at a conference.'

'It ended early.'

A badly organized conference.

Salas was as impolitely abrupt as ever. 'Have you the slightest idea of what a full analysis of evidence costs?'

'Not really, Señor.'

'Yet you send a bottle of whisky and some glasses to the Laboratory of Forensic Sciences and demand one such without the authority to do so?'

'I judged that speed of action was essential.'

'A most unusual judgement for you to make.'

'In this case . . .'

'What case?'

'The disappearance of the Englishman, Señor Neil Lewis.'

'I have read through all the reports received during my absence and cannot recall one dealing with this matter.'

'I haven't yet made a preliminary report because so many of the facts are still uncertain.'

If uncertain, how do you begin to justify your request for a full analysis at exorbitant cost to the department?'

'Because I think that the results will establish that Lewis was murdered. I believe some form of narcotic was introduced into the unopened bottle of whisky . . .'

'It clearly has not occurred to you that if a bottle is unopened, nothing can have been introduced into it.'

'When I said unopened, señor, I meant it appeared to be, but wasn't. How much effort did Señor Lewis have to use in order to unscrew the cap? If he had to use a degree of force . . .'

'Did he?'

'I cannot determine that fact.'

'Are there any facts you have determined?'

'When the three woke up on the boat . . .'

'What three, what boat?'

'Lewis and Sheard met two young women in the port and after a few drinks went for a trip in the boat Lewis had chartered. They anchored off the Hotel Parelona, emptied one bottle of whisky, opened another and had a drink before they began to have fun . . .'

'What do you mean by that expression?'

'Well, they started fondling each other and undressing . . .'

'Are you quite incapable of investigating a case without introducing sex into it?'

'I am only reporting what happened, señor.'

'Using the word "fun" makes it very obvious that you do so without the sense of distaste I expect from my officers.'

'I am sorry, señor. They were indulging in amorous foreplay . . .'

'Are you trying to be obscenely humorous?'

'No, señor. That is what it is sometimes called.'

'By those of a like mind to you.'

'Then they fell asleep. It seems so unusual a moment to fall asleep in view of the . . .'

'Restrain your urge to wallow in unnecessary and unsavoury details.'

Alvarez briefly detailed the facts.

'You have no reason to suspect involvement in the drug trade other than the Englishman's sudden accession of wealth?'

'That and the nature of his disappearance.'

'As to the latter, would it not be reasonable to suppose he was so drunk that he fell over the side and drowned?'

'The evidence is that he wasn't drunk.'

'Evidence given by his companions who would have been as drunk as he.'

'Señorita Glass says she had had very little.'

'Women are recognized to have an infinite capacity for self-delusion.'

'But even if he was tight, he was a very strong swimmer.'

'A man can be so intoxicated that he becomes incapable of doing something which he does easily and well when sober.'

'If he were too drunk even to remember how to swim, could he have walked out of the saloon on to the deck and across to the stern? Would he have bothered to in order to urinate?'

'I am glad to say it is not a question I can answer. Have you traced the source of the money?'

'Not yet.'

'Why not?'

'The banks are checking, but they say it'll take time.'

'Can you name anything on this island that does not take twice as long as is reasonable?' He rang off.

Alvarez replaced the receiver. If only Salas had remained at the conference until at least some of the facts could have been established with a degree of certainty . . . If every 'if' were a peseta, no man would be poor.

CHAPTER EIGHT

The phone rang as he was about to leave the office for his merienda of a coffee and brandy at the Club Llueso.

'It's the Guardia, phoning from Torret. We've a dead man, in his twenties, in what's almost certainly a hit-and-run.'

'Torret's in Inspector Cardona's territory,'

he said with satisfaction.

'We called him and he's worked out that as the body is six kilometres to the east of the village, it's just in yours.'

Some would do anything to evade their responsibilities, he thought resentfully.

*   *   *

The road, which over the past two kilometres had become a switchback, turned sharp right round a bluff of exposed rock, then bore sharply down in a left-hand curve before levelling off. Evergreen oaks cast their shadows on the road and fields of almond trees stretched almost to the mountains. It was a part of the island with very little underground water so that only one crop a year could be grown to augment the almonds.

Alvarez parked behind the white and green Renault, walked up to the driver's door. The two cabos remained seated, enjoying the slight relief from the heat that the car's fan provided. The driver spoke through the open window. 'He went off the road down by the second telegraph pole.'

Alvarez saw that a cistus bush immediately to the side of the pole had been partially flattened. 'What was he riding?'

'A Vespa. That's been caught up a metre or so below the level of the road. From the look of things, a car coming up behind didn't see it in time and smacked it over. There's a fair drop on to rock and the poor sod landed on his head—wasn't wearing a crash helmet.'

'Do we know when the accident happened?'

'The doc says rigor was fully established and that, plus body temperature, suggested twelve hours from death, only in this heat nothing could be certain.'

'Where's the body?'

'With the village undertakers.'

'Do we have identification?'

'There was none on him and a check with Traffic gives the Vespa as owned by a bloke in Palma. He's been contacted and says he sold it last year, but just didn't bother with the paperwork for the transfer.'

'Have any locals been reported missing?'

'None we've heard about.'

Alvarez walked down the road. A short distance from the cistus bush, there was a mark on the tarmac where something had recently scraped along the surface with considerable force. He reached the bush and looked down and immediately wished he hadn't. The land was steeper than seemed likely from the road and there was a sloping fall of some seven metres. At the point where the Vespa had been held by a projecting rock, the land fell less steeply than elsewhere, nevertheless he would not have dreamt of climbing down had not there been two cabos ready to jeer at him if he did not.

It was an old machine, in parts rusty, and now slightly bent though far from wrecked. It was difficult to disagree with the conclusion that a car coming up from behind had hit the Vespa and knocked it on to its side with such force that it had swept along the road to fall over the edge; yet the rear of the machine had not suffered the crumpling he would have expected to find in such an accident.

Careful only to look up, never down, he climbed back to the road. He walked up to the car. 'Call Traffic to collect the Vespa and take it to Palma for a full vehicle examination.'

'What's to prevent you telling 'em?' asked the driver bad-temperedly.

He carried on to his own car and drove off.

Torret, originally built about a hill for defensive purposes, had altered little, largely because it was well back from the coast and few foreigners ever visited it, even fewer lived there—those who did were of strange persuasions, some of which even the accommodating locals would have baulked at had they known about them. It was a village of uneven levels, narrow streets mostly without pavements, a church with a relic of St Boniface, a band which could play four and a half tunes, and a yearly fight between Moors and Christians of such violence that in some years there were almost as many casualties as tradition claimed for the original battle (which some historians were so insensitive as to claim never occurred).

He parked in the main square and walked across to a bar which was built against one wall of the church, a juxtaposition the Latin character found perfectly natural. He ordered a coffee and a brandy, then said to the owner: 'Where will I find the undertaker?'

'At the edge of the village, on the Palma road. Moved there a couple of years back . . . You sound like you're from Llueso? '

'That's right.'

'Can't mistake the accent!'

'The purest Mallorquin,' Alvarez responded, automatically defending the good name of his village.

'I've a cousin who lives there, Lucia, married to Gustavo, a carpenter.'

'I've had a word or two with him, but I've not met her.'

'The last time she was here, she said Gustavo's very successful. Could that be right?'

'He's moved into specially built workshops just outside the village and is doing cabinet-making as well as ordinary work. They say that last year he won a prestigious prize in the Barcelona exhibition.'

'Is that right! If Lucía's mother had lived to now, I wonder what she'd have to say. When Lucia told her she was marrying a man from Llueso, she had hysterics and burned candles by the score to try and stop it . . . You never can tell, can you?'

'Not until it's too late to do anything about things.'

The owner moved away to serve another customer. Alvarez spooned sugar into the cup, drank some of the coffee, emptied the brandy into what remained. The Vergers would have married at least thirty-five years before. Then, Torret had, as had many inland villages, been relatively isolated, not only physically but also psychologically, so that Lucia's mother's hostility towards the marriage was understandable. Then, ignorance had often fuelled traditional rivalries; it had been a source of pride that the vocabulary of one village was noticeably different from that of another. Here a wife could plough, there to do so was to earn as much shame as if she were a puta ... Easy travel and television had homogenized the island, thereby eliminating those fears and prejudices born of ignorance, but at a price that still couldn't be accurately calculated. It would be ironic if when the price did become known, it would be seen that there had been merit in ignorance ...

He left the bar and returned to his car, drove through the steep, narrow, winding streets to the undertaker's house and offices—the latter tastefully camouflaged as an ordinary extension.

The undertaker was short and tubby, and he had a mobile face which could register whatever degree of mournful compassion seemed appropriate. 'You believe you may be a relative?'

'Cuerpo General de Policia.'

'You have papers of authority to confirm that fact?'

'Never bother to carry 'em around.'

'Then I regret I cannot permit you to view the deceased.'

'Did he present his papers in order that you could accept him?'

'Only a genuine policeman could say anything so ridiculous!' He led the way through an inner doorway into a tiled room and crossed to one of four refrigerated cabinets, disengaged the locking bars, and pulled out a shelf. 'His cranial injuries are very considerable.'

They were, but Alvarez had no difficulty in recognizing Sheard.

CHAPTER NINE

Alvarez watched a gecko scurry across the ceiling, then come to an abrupt halt a few centimetres away from the corner. Such action often indicated a potential victim had been sighted, yet he could see no fly or spider and it seemed possible the gecko had been tricked by the light into believing it had seen movement. Perhaps he, too, was being tricked into believing he was seeing connections where there was none.

A detective quickly learned that coincidences were commonplace, yet when faced by one his first reaction was almost invariably to dismiss the possibility that it was genuine. So here he was, trying to identify the connection between the presumed death of Lewis and the death of Sheard, when it could be pure coincidence that one had died within four days of the other.

The telephone rang.

'This is Benito Vinent, manager of the Annuig branch of Sa Nostra. A day or two ago, I received a request for information concerning a foreigner, probably English-speaking, who had made a heavy withdrawal in cash in the past two weeks. I have information regarding such a withdrawal, but before going any further, I need to satisfy myself that the proper procedure has been observed. You have obtained the necessary permission to request and be given such information?' He spoke with old-fashioned formality that was leavened with a touch of irony, as if he were smiling at himself.

'It would not occur to me', Alvarez answered reproachfully, 'to act before I had done so.'

'I'm sorry that I was obliged to ask.'

'Think nothing of it.'

'On the twenty-fifth of last month, Señor Clough presented a cheque in sterling for a large sum. He has not banked with us for long,

64

but since he has shown himself to be a valued client, his account was immediately credited with that sum in pesetas. He withdrew one million in cash.'

Alvarez searched amongst the sprawl of papers on his desk and found the one he wanted. Lewis had left Sheard's room on the twenty-sixth to move into the Hotel Vista Bella. 'What is Señor Clough's address?'

'Son Preda.'

'That is all?'

'It is a manorial house a couple of kilometres outside the village and so there is no need for any more. I know that even dirt tracks are being named and signposted these days—will they never cease to find ways of wasting our money?—but I've no idea of the name of the lane Son Preda is on.'

'Is Señor Clough English?'

'What other nationality so delights in a language which sunders pronunciation from spelling?'

'What kind of a man is he?'

'It is difficult for me to judge since he speaks almost no Spanish and I speak barely any more English and we have to converse through one of my staff. All I can answer is that he is friendly and has a ready sense of humour.'

'Is he married?'

'He is.'

'Any family?'

'None has been mentioned.'

'Then that's about it. Thanks for your help.'

'One moment, Inspector. I should like to ask a favour. Can you indicate whether I might, perhaps, be mistaken when I believe the señor to be a valued client for the bank?'

'All I know about him is what you've just told me. The only reason I'm asking questions is that, having identified him, he may be able to help me in investigations concerning an Englishman who has disappeared from a boat and is presumed drowned.'

'An answer that would seem to leave room for considerable ambiguity.'

'Don't most?'

'I think I will make a call to head office to confirm that the señor's cheque has been cleared.'

Alvarez rang off, began to doodle on the corner of a sheet of paper. If one were travelling from Port Llueso to Annuig there were two possible routes, one of which went through Torret. Clough had withdrawn a million pesetas the day before Lewis moved into the hotel. Just two more coincidences? The shepherd who found his flock constantly diminishing soon counted the sheep in his neighbours' fields.

*   *   *

Son Preda had been owned by the same family for many generations. It was a large estate

66

which encompassed both rich, fertile land and bleak mountainside. When labour had been cheap, up to thirty men had been employed full time, as many again part time at the busiest periods of the year. It had been almost self-supporting. Pigs, sheep, cattle, mules, goats, chickens, ducks, and pigeons had been reared; oil had been pressed from the ripe olives; figs had been sun-dried for both human and animal consumption; almonds had either been sold and the proceeds used for the few things needed from the outside or turned into turrótn for a Xmas treat; cheese had been made with the help of vine leaves; wheat had been milled and the bread baked in 'Roman' ovens, fired by wood; oranges, lemons, grapefruit, pomegranates, loquats, cherries, pears, apples, tomatoes, peas, beans, cabbages, cauliflowers, lettuces, aubergines, sweet peppers, carrots, radishes, melons, and grapes had been grown; wine had been made; after summer rains, stone walls had been searched for snails; in January or February, shivering men had climbed the tallest mountain and cut out squares of snow which had been stored in the snow house to provide the supreme luxury of cold in the big heat . . .

Then tourism had arrived. Wages had risen until self-sufficiency ceased to be an admirable objective and became an impossible luxury. The style of government had changed and democratic taxes had been introduced with the declared objective of preventing the rich living off the backs of the poor—as one wag had remarked, before long, the poor were living off the livers of the rich . . .

But although Son Preda could no longer live in the past, its owner had decided it must survive to live in the future. Fortunate still to be wealthy because he was advised by an expert in identifying tax loopholes, he had invested much money in restoring, altering, and adapting. The land was cultivated by a few men and many machines. The very large, two-hundred-year-old house was carefully modernized and then let to whoever was willing to pay the very high rent . . .

Alvarez braked to a stop in front of several stone steps leading up to a wooden door patterned with wrought-iron studs and striated by decade after decade of changing weather. As he stepped on to the gravel and looked up at the four-storey building, he was momentarily taken back to his childhood when the owner of such a house possessed an authority little less than God's.

He climbed the steps. On the door was a huge wrought-iron knocker in the shape of a ring hanging from a bull's nose, while set in the stonework to the side was an electric bell push. Ever the traditionalist, he chose the knocker. The sound it made against the wood was the beat of past centuries.

The door, hinges squealing, was swung back

68

and he faced a woman in maid's uniform, who looked as if she didn't need to call for a man if a heavy weight needed lifting. 'Is Señor Clough here?'

She studied him. 'And if he is?' she finally demanded.

'I want to talk to him. Inspector Alvarez, Cuerpo General de Policia.'

'I suppose you'd better come in, then,' she said bad-temperedly.

He entered a very large hall, somewhat sparsely furnished. She led the way into the room immediately on the left.

He looked around. The furniture was modern, better quality Mallorquin. Above the carved mantelpiece was a painting of a couple in traditional dress, the man playing Mallorquin bagpipes; ranged along the wall on either side were flintlock rifles. In a mahogany bookcase—almost certainly foreign—were a large number of uniformly bound volumes that had the dusty look of books respected but seldom read. On the tiled floor was a large carpet that to judge from the crude patterns and colours had been made in the local factory before it had been forced to close many years before because of the cheaper and more sophisticatedly patterned carpets which had come in from the Peninsula.

He heard a sound and turned to see a man enter. 'Señor Clough? I'm sorry to bother you, but I wish to ask some questions.'

'You speak English! A necessary prerequisite to my understanding the questions, let alone answering them.' He was tall, well shouldered, and had a trim waist; his dark hair was thick and neatly trimmed; his face was oval, his eyebrows marked, his nose aquiline, his mouth full and firm, his jaw square; he had a moustache, not so small as to look an affectation, not so overgrown as to be ridiculous. He wore an open-neck shirt and fawn flannels which possessed the quality, which only money could buy, of being both casual and smart.

A man who could be as sharp as he was pleasant, was Alvarez's immediate assumption. Also one who was showing the touch of condescension that so many English did. This caused him no resentment. The man who condescended often failed to look where he was treading. 'I will try to be as brief as possible, señor.'

'There's no call to rush. Sit down and let me get you something to drink before you tell me what the problem is. What would you like?'

'May I have a coñac, please, with just ice.'

Clough left the room, to return with a tray on which were two glasses. He handed one to Alvarez, lifted up the second, put the tray down on a stool, sat. 'Your good health.'

'And yours, señor.'

Clough drank. 'Do you smoke?'

'Occasionally, despite the doctor's advice.'

70

'Ignore that. Doctors spend their lives wrestling with other people's problems so they lead a miserable life and their only relief is to try to make everyone else's life equally miserable. There are cigarettes in the box by your side.'

Alvarez opened the chased silver box, brought out a cigarette, lit this with the small silver lighter to the side of the box.

'Tell me, Inspector, have I inadvertently broken one of the many thousands of rules and regulations?'

'Nothing like that, señor. I just need to discover if you have been acquainted with two people.'

'Their names?'

'Neil Lewis is the first.'

'I knew a Mark Lewis, but that was back in England ten years ago and, after he and his wife split up, I don't think I ever saw him again. My wife was very fond of Angela and inevitably during the break-up started seeing things from her point of view, which naturally upset Mark. It's a sad fact that it's virtually impossible to stay friendly with both sides. But then there isn't much room for neutrality anywhere, is there? . . . All of which has absolutely nothing to do with your Neil Lewis. No, we have not knowingly met anyone by that name, although I can't say for certain because at parties one is never quite sure whom one has met.'

'He was on holiday in Port Llueso and on

71

Thursday night disappeared from a boat anchored in the bay. There's been no sight of him since, so it has to be presumed that he drowned.'

'I'm sorry to hear that. Couldn't swim, I suppose. It really is quite extraordinary how many presumably intelligent people set sail on boats without a second thought when they can't swim a stroke.'

'I understand he was a strong swimmer.'

'Then why did he drown?'

'That is a question I am trying to answer.'

'I'm sorry, but I can't help you ... What made you think I might have known him?'

'He arrived in the port in the middle of last month and had very little money, yet eight days later booked in at one of the more expensive hotels and chartered a motor boat.'

'The Midas touch.'

'On the twenty-fifth of last month, you paid a large sterling cheque into your bank. On the same day, you withdrew a million pesetas in cash.'

'The cost of living is like the arrow of time, it has only one direction.' His tone sharpened. 'Am I allowed to know how you became cognizant of these facts?'

'When we can show this to be necessary to a major investigation, we have the right to ask a bank to breach the rules on customer secrecy. Surely the police have a similar right in your country?'

'Of course. But how could there be such a necessity when, as I've just said, I have never knowingly met the unfortunate man? In any case, since when has an accidental drowning been rated a major crime?'

'As I have suggested, there is the possibility that the señor's death was not the result of an accident. Until all the surrounding facts are known, it will not be possible to be certain.'

Clough said: 'It seems we have something of a Catch-22 situation. You are required to show that a crime has been committed in order to gain permission for the disclosure of bank account details; you demand the details of an account in order to establish there has been a crime.'

'What did you do with the million pesetas?'

'What does one normally do with money?'

'Even today, such a large amount...' He stopped as the door opened and a woman entered.

She came to a halt just inside the room. 'Julia said we had a visitor from the police...' She became silent.

Clough rose. 'Inspector Alvarez. Inspector, my wife.'

Belatedly, Alvarez remembered that the English had the strange habit of coming to their feet when a woman first entered the room and he hastily stood. 'It is a pleasure to meet you, señora.' Since experience suggested that the richer the husband, the younger and more glamorous the current wife, he was surprised by the fact that she was roughly Clough's age, far from glamorous, and dressed for comfort, not effect.

'Do sit,' Clough said. 'Standing raises one nearer heaven, but can be hell on the legs ... Vera, the inspector is asking if we know a Neil Lewis. I've told him, the only Lewis we've ever known is Mark and it's years since we last had contact.'

She settled on the settee. 'Why ... What's happened?'

'This Lewis has fallen from a boat and has to be presumed drowned.'

'Oh, no!'

Alvarez was surprised by the degree of her distress.

Clough, his tone one of ironic resignation, said: 'As you can judge, Inspector, every man's death certainly diminishes my wife! In fact, she suffers other people's misfortunes more than her own.'

Her manner had seemed to suggest a more than general concern over a tragedy that had overtaken a stranger; Clough had been very quick to explain away her reaction. 'Señora, I have to try and find out how and why it happened.'

'Of course,' she murmured.

'Perhaps you won't mind helping me?'

'I'm curious,' Clough said. 'How can my wife begin to help you when she has never met the

74

unfortunate man, hasn't been on our boat in the past fortnight, and was last in Llueso several days ago?'

'Sometimes, señor, a negative can be useful.'

'Then you'll undoubtedly find what she has to say very useful indeed!'

Alvarez turned to face Vera. 'Your husband has told me that he does not know anyone by the name of Neil Lewis . . .

Clough interrupted him. 'I said, *we* do not.'

'You are quite right, señor. However, I should be grateful if the señora would confirm that she has never met anyone of that name.'

After a moment, she said, in a low voice: 'No, I haven't.'

'Have you ever met a man called Albert Sheard?'

'No.'

It had been a much stronger denial.

'Who is Sheard?' Cough asked. 'Was he also aboard the boat and has disappeared, to be presumed drowned?'

'Last night he was riding a Vespa when he was knocked down by a car and died from his injuries.'

'Very soon, you'll have my wife inconsolable!'

'It's all so terrible,' she said.

Her words had lacked emotion; it was as if they had been spoken to her husband's cue. 'Señor, did you know Albert Sheard?'

'No. Have you the slightest reason for

thinking either of us might have done?'

'He and Señor Lewis were friends.'

'Hardly of consequence in the present context.'

'Señor Sheard's crash occurred on the road between Port Llueso and Torret.'

'So?'

'It is one of the two routes one would take to reach here.'

'You are trying to say he may have been coming here?'

'It seems a possibility.'

'Only by stretching the laws of possibilities to breaking point. Tell me, do you pursue your logic to its logical conclusion? Is every person who was on that road, and on the alternative one, to be considered a potential visitor to Son Preda?'

'Only if that person had a reason for meeting you.'

'I am intrigued. What are you now going to suggest was Sheard's reason for meeting me, a complete stranger?'

'I'm not certain. But it may have had a connection with the money you withdrew.'

'Ah, yes! Your concern just before my wife came in.' Clough turned to Vera. 'The inspector has been showing considerable interest in our financial affairs, to the extent of persuading the bank to divulge details of our account. It seems my withdrawal of a million pesetas a fortnight ago troubles him. From his inability to judge a wife's capacity to spend, it's my guess he's not married.' He turned back. 'Are you, in fact, married?'

'No, Señor.'

'Your incomprehension becomes comprehensible. I will explain. Some little time ago, we were invited to stay in the near future with friends for whom form is all-important. My wife normally dresses without fuss or frills, but there are occasions when she has to accept the necessity of doing otherwise and this will be one such. So that is why I have had to rediscover the fact that a couple of dresses can cost as much as a man's entire wardrobe.'

Alvarez asked her: 'You have bought some dresses on the island, señora?'

She looked to her husband.

He said: 'Whenever my wife needs something special to wear, she has it made by a dressmaker in England.'

'Are you saying that the million pesetas was needed to pay this dressmaker?'

'Indeed.'

'Even though she works in England and one would expect her to be paid in pounds?'

'Correct again.'

'Would you be kind enough to show me her receipt.' Alvarez did not miss the sudden look of consternation on Vera's face.

Clough showed no such concern. 'Your justification for the request?'

'The receipt would confirm what you've just

77

told me.'

'You need confirmation?'

'Regretfully, in my job I have to seek confirmation of everything I am told.'

'Seek but, presumably, do not always find?'

'May I see the receipt?'

'I have to disappoint you.'

'Why?'

'Basically, because the dressmaker is a talented woman of much common sense—the two, of course, do not always go together.'

'I don't understand.'

'She is employed by one of the larger London ateliers and it is a condition of her employment that she works for no one else. Therefore, she never gives a receipt for work done on the side, since this could incriminate her and lead to her dismissal. Further, it was she who suggested she delivered the dresses here, not London, so that she could be paid in pesetas. I imagine she is buying a property, but naturally didn't ask. We were delighted to agree. It saved my wife making a journey to the UK.'

'What is her name and address?'

Clough smiled. 'Give those and she runs the risk of having her moonlighting identified by the Inland Revenue, which would be small thanks for all her care. No, Inspector, I will not give you those details. Were I to do so and as a direct consequence she was in trouble and unable to carry out further commissions for my wife, I should never be forgiven by eithe. party.'

Alvarez felt a certain admiration for the other. He could not have expected to be questioned; the questions could well have caused a sense of panic; yet he had thought up, on the spur of the moment, answers that were just this side of feasible and offered a valid reason for not providing corroborative evidence. It was not every man who was that quick of thought.

'Have you any more questions?'

'I don't think so, señor.'

'Then we can relax and I'll get you another drink.'

Alvarez saw no reason to refuse.

CHAPTER TEN

Alvarez was awoken by Dolores's call. He stared up at the bedroom ceiling and decided that after winning the lottery, he'd pay someone to wake him up at the end of every siesta so that he could enjoy the luxury of returning to sleep.

'Are you up, Enrique?'

He slowly and reluctantly swivelled round, put his bare feet on the floor, and rested. Sweat trickled down his chest.

'Hurry up. Your coffee's getting cold.'

She was forever fussing. Perhaps somewhere in her ancestry there was a Galician influence. He stood. By ill chance he was standing at right angles to the small mirror on the chest of drawers and could see his stomach. Another few centimetres and he would be forced to accept the description, fat. He really must, he decided resolutely, go on a diet.

Dolores should not have offered him a second slice of almond cake. After all, it would have hurt her feelings to refuse ... He gathered up the few crumbs left on the plate, pressed them together between thumb and forefinger, put them in his mouth and savoured their flavour ...

'You're going to be really late,' she said.

He looked up at the electric clock on the wall and was surprised to note that the time was almost six. 'Is it easy to spend a million pesetas on two frocks?'

'Madness, more like!'

'Sure. But are there people who spend that much?'

'I've read there are some who waste even more to look ridiculous.'

Was Vera Clough one such person? From what he'd seen of her, he doubted that whatever the occasion she would dress ostentatiously, yet accepted that it was dangerous on so brief an acquaintance to make any judgement, let alone one that only a woman could correctly make. Nevertheless, one developed an instinct about a case and his said the story of the dresses was nonsense . . . Vera Clough had been shocked by the news of Lewis's death, but not by Sheard's—obviously, people were far more concerned over the death of someone known than someone unknown to them . . . Would she have accepted from her husband the need to deny any meeting with Lewis unless there was very good reason for the denial? If she accepted the need, she must have a good idea of what her husband was doing . . .

'Are you all right?' Dolores asked.

He looked up to see her standing at the head of the table and regarding him intently. 'Why d'you ask?'

'You're very late for work, yet you just sit there and stare into space.'

'I'm trying to decide whether the latest case I'm on is connected with drugs.'

She began to fidget with the wooden spoon that was on the table. 'Ana's eldest has been stealing money from the family. When she found this out and asked him why, he told her he was on drugs. Yet no one could have been brought up in a more loving family. Why? Why should he do such a terrible thing?'

'Home life doesn't seem to carry the weight it used to. The experts talk about peer pressure, the excitement of taking risks and breaking the law.'

'Experts are idiots! It's because the government changed the law and

81

decriminalized drugs.'

'Governments are bigger idiots than experts.'

'It was different in General Franco's time.'

'Many things were different.'

'When I hear about Ana's eldest, I think of Juan and Isabel.'

'They'll never take to drugs.'

'Why not, if a loving home is no guarantee? Why should they listen to us rather than some piece of shit who wants to see them hooked?' The strength of her fears was evidenced by her language; normally, she never swore.

'They are sensible.'

'And that is enough?'

'With the help of God.'

'Does He not permit there to be such terrible drugs? Does He not permit the old to tempt the young? So why should He help?'

'Why not ask the priest?' he said, ducking an answer.

'How can he understand the fears of a mother when he does not know what it is to have children?'

'He'll have been taught to give advice on matters he cannot experience.'

'And would you go to a chemist to be told how to build a house?'

Again, he did not try to answer.

'You must know who are the local bastards— why don't you arrest them?'

'I need evidence and there's never enough to

catch the people who really matter,' he said sadly. It needed a cleverer man than he to understand why the law allowed itself to be used by criminals to evade justice.

'There were no drugs before the foreigners came. There was no pornography. You left the house unlocked when you went out. Families stayed together and the young supported the old. The foreigners should never have been allowed here.'

'Then you would be cooking on charcoal.'

'A small price to pay.'

Since her cooking would still be superb, she was probably correct.

*   *   *

Alvarez considered the problem. The rules were clear, Any request for information to a foreign police force, normally passed through Interpol, had to be approved by someone of the rank of comisario or higher. To reach the rank of comisario, a man had to have ambition; an ambitious man did not make the mistake of helping a colleague if to do so carried the slightest element of risk. Yet if he didn't ask one of the comisarios to endorse the request, that left only Salas. And there could be no doubt as to how he would react to the suggestion . . . Of course, if the request to the English police for information, both formal and informal, concerning Lawrence Clough and Neil Lewis, appeared to have the superior chief's authority and if it asked that such information be sent direct to Llueso, why should Salas ever have cause to object? A man did not bemoan a lost lamb until he knew he had lost it.

* * *

He parked, locked the car, walked the short distance to the Hotel Alhambra. In the foyer, suitcases and hold-alls were piled high, men and women were milling about the reception desk, and children were racing, shouting, and screaming. A typical change-over day. The two harassed clerks ignored him until he leaned across the reception desk and announced himself.

'Can't it wait?' asked the older plaintively.

'I'm afraid not.'

'Twenty bodies arriving when only eighteen were expected and only eighteen beds vacated. Where am I to put the extra two?'

A woman with a sharply featured face and tight, thin mouth pushed her way past Alvarez. She said stridently: 'All right, when are you going to do something instead of being pathetic?'

The elder receptionist spoke in a placatory voice. 'Señora, we are trying . . .'

'Very trying! I've been waiting for hours and all you've done is chat to him.' She indicated

Alvarez with an indignant jerk of her head.

'But I have to speak to him, Señora . . .'

'You find me and my husband a room quick sharp or I'm suing the company in England.'

'Please wait one little moment . . .'

'Wait? That's all this bloody place is good for.'

Alvarez said in English: 'We have a saying, Señora. The man who runs often arrives after the man who walks.'

'You speak a little English, do you? Well I'm telling you, there's not much running done on this island, that's for sure. No one's doing anything about finding a bedroom for me and my husband. Booked it three months ago. Three months! And then they try to say there ain't a bedroom free. If they expect us to sleep on the sand, they've got another bloody great think coming their way, that's for sure!'

The elder receptionist leaned forward. 'Señora, I assure you that you will not have to wait for much longer.'

'Maybe I won't if you stop chatting to this bloke and do your job.'

'But it is a police matter, Señor Alvarez is a detective.'

The woman studied Alvarez. Her expression made it clear that he did not look like one.

'Do you get many like this?' Alvarez asked in Mallorquin.

'Always some. And when they get tight, they're even worse . . . Tell me quickly what

85

you want.'

'Is Señorita Fenn or Señorita Glass in the hotel?'

The receptionist checked. 'Their key isn't hanging up so I guess at least one of them's around.'

'What's the room number?'

'Sixteen. First floor, turn right from the lift.'

Alvarez eased his way past the glowering woman and crossed to the lift. As he entered, three boys rushed in, deafened him with a ghetto blaster, shouted, 'Hey, old man, hit the tit for take-off,' pressed the button for the fourth floor, then fooled around. After reaching the fourth floor, they stomped their way out of the lift. He was able to descend to the first floor.

He knocked on the door of room 16 and there was a call from inside to enter. The two single beds filled the small room; Kirsty, wearing a bikini, was lying on the right-hand one. She sat up. 'Have you learned something?'

'Concerning Señor Lewis? I regret not.'

'Oh! I've been so hoping . . .'

She was genuinely concerned, not because convention demanded this.

'Is Señorita Fenn in the hotel?'

'No, she's out with . . . with a friend.' She noticed his expression. 'She was so upset she needed taking out of herself.'

'Señorita, would you mind if I sat?' He settled on the other bed since there was no

86

chair. 'I fear I have more bad news for you.'

'Oh, God!'

'Late yesterday evening, Señor Sheard was riding his Vespa when he had a serious crash. Sadly, he died from his injuries.'

She turned her head away, but not before he had seen the look of shock that distorted her features. After a while, she said in a small voice: 'It was going to be a wonderful holiday. We were going to have such fun. But . . . Why does it happen?'

'No one knows.'

After a while, she turned back, eyes reddened, cheeks damp. 'I've been wondering why he didn't come and tell us what was happening; we haven't seen him since Sunday. I just thought it must be because he was so shocked. I mean, him and Neil were pals . . . Could it be because he was so upset that he had the accident? It happens like that, doesn't it?'

'I'm sure it does. But, señorita, at the moment there is no certainty that it was an accident.'

'How d'you mean? Here, you're surely not saying it was deliberate?'

'I am trying to find out what were the circumstances.'

'You mean, it could've been? Oh, God, it's a curse, like the one when they opened that tomb in Egypt. First Neil, then Bert. Next . . .'

'I can assure you that neither Señorita Fenn

nor you have any need for fear.'

She began to pluck at a fold in the bedspread.

'I am here to find out if you can help me discover the truth.'

'But how can I?'

'You did not know the señors for long, but during the time you did, they must have spoken about many things and they may have said something that will help me. Was there ever any mention of drugs?'

'Are you saying they was into that?'

'It is one of the many possibilities I have to explore. Did they, perhaps, offer you a reefer when you were on the boat?'

'No. And if they had, I'd have told them what to do with it . . . Look, we was having fun, but nothing like that. Dope is different. I've friends what are really hooked and if I was like them I'd want to cut my throat. They never suggested reefers, coke, E, happies, anything.'

He judged her to be telling the truth. 'Did Señor Lewis or Señor Sheard ever mention the name Lawrence Clough?'

She shook her head. Then she said: 'Hang on.' She thought back, her forehead creased. 'Larry's short for Lawrence and I think I remember someone mentioning Larry . . . That's it. We'd anchored and was having the first drink. Neil was fooling around with Cara and was talking like men do when they're trying to get you to agree—know what I mean?'

Did she really judge him to be so ancient he did not?

'Neil was busy with his hands and she was trying to stop him going too fast and he said he'd fallen for her so heavy that he'd give her anything she wanted. She said he could take her for a holiday in Bali. Last year she read about how wonderful the place is and hasn't stopped telling everyone she wants to go there. But as I said to her before we came here, Port Llueso's the nearest she's ever going to get to Bali. She told Neil this and he got a bit narked because I'd kind of made him look stupid and he said I didn't begin to know my way around the world. All he had to do was have a word with Larry and he'd be able to take Cara to Bali, Hawaii, Hollywood, and New York.'

'Did he explain how Larry could help him do all these things?'

She shook her head.

He stood. 'Thank you, señorita.'

'I told you I don't know anything.'

'On the contrary, what you've just said may help me considerably.'

'It may?'

Unless he was seeing a flock of goats where there was not even a kid, Lewis had unthinkingly confirmed the fact that Lawrence Clough had been bankrolling him.

CHAPTER ELEVEN

Traffic reported late on Wednesday morning.

'The Vespa's an interesting little puzzle. There are no hard scrapes, no smears of foreign paint, as there normally are when two vehicles collide; the damage to the front mudguard and left-hand foot rest and the impacted earth are consistent with the Vespa sliding along the road, off on to the verge, and down the slope. The tyres, especially the front one, are badly worn and with very little tread. There's a dent in the rear mudguard, but apparently of little consequence. So the picture seems to be of a bike that's not looked after and a driver who loses control and skids. But the road was bone dry and the marks on it say the bike wasn't moving fast. So why should the rider suddenly lose control?

'Suppose it wasn't an accident. The easiest way to ensure a powered bike crashes is to come up behind in a car and push hard against the rear mudguard at an angle. Get it right and the driver hasn't a hope in hell. But with that scenario, there's crushed and powdered paintwork on the bike and usually the mudguard is pushed hard into the tyre. The Vespa has no crushed paintwork, no scrapes down to the metal, and only a small dent in the mudguard. Which calls to mind the old dodge of lashing an old outer tyre on to the car's front bumper. Then, if the driver is careful, there's little or no crushing and powdering, no scraping, and only slight denting. Afterwards, the tyre is burned and so there are no traces on the car to identify it ... We used special techniques to examine the mudguard and although it was very faint, we think we found a small piece of a tread pattern.'

'You only think?'

'I'm afraid we can't be more definite.'

After the call was over, Alvarez settled back in the chair.

If there had been a reason to murder Sheard, it was a hundred to one he had been murdered; but until that was established, there was no certainty that there was a reason.

He phoned the Laboratory of Forensic Sciences and asked if they had the results of their analyses of the whisky and the residues in the two glasses he had sent them. Their reply was to be expected. Did he think they had nothing to do but the work he sent them? Did he think they worked twenty-four hours a day? Did he believe ...

Exhausted by their aggressive hostility, so clearly aimed at concealing their indolence, he leaned over and pulled open the right-hand bottom drawer of the desk and brought out a bottle of brandy and a glass.

*　　　*　　　*

One possible lead was to discover if there were

any rumours on the streets of an English intrusion into the drug market. Alvarez drove down to the port and went into one of the backstreet bars. He was in luck. Capella sat at one of the tables, playing a game of draughts.

Capella was a small man, not quite as old as he looked; his pointed face and sharp, beady eyes had given him his nickname, Ferret. His right arm hung uselessly at his side. Thirty years before he had suffered a bad fall, but had been unable to seek medical help because the Guardia had ordered all doctors and hospitals to advise them if they treated a man of his description with an injured arm.

As Alvarez approached, both players looked up briefly; Capella muttered a greeting, Obrador merely nodded. They played on, but after three more moves, Obrador swore, accepted defeat, pushed a five-hundred-peseta coin across the table, and left.

'He seemed to lose his concentration,' Alvarez said.

'What d'you expect, turning up and staring at him?'

'Then how about recognizing my assistance by giving me half your winnings?'

Capella hurriedly pocketed the coin.

'What are you drinking?'

'Nothing.'

Alvarez picked up the glass in front of Capella, crossed to the bar and ordered two brandies. Filled glasses in his hands, he returned, sat. 'So what's he into these days? Cigarettes? I hear things have become very difficult, with supplies from Tangiers and Ceuta drying up and the authorities becoming sharper. Not like the old days, when you could make enough in one good run to build yourself a house and another for your daughter.'

'The money was left me by an uncle.'

'Tio Andrés? He never left anyone anything but curses.'

'What gives you the right to slander the dead?'

'His curses.' Alvarez offered the other a cigarette, lit a match for both of them. 'Tell me all about the drug scene here in the port.'

'You think I have anything to do with that?'

'No. But you'll know what's going on because you still keep your ear so close to the ground you have perpetual earache. Have there been any changes just recently?'

Capella drained his glass, put it down on the table with more force than was necessary. Alvarez carried both glasses to the bar and had them refilled. He returned. 'Well?'

'What d'you mean, changes?'

'Are the English moving in?'

'You think the lads would let 'em?'

'Not without causing trouble.'

'There ain't been any.'

'Are you sure?'

''Course I'm sure,' Capella retorted, ignoring the fact that only a moment ago he'd claimed not to know what was happening.

'You don't think they could be working so quietly they're even using their own boat?'

'The day after it sailed, it'd be at the bottom and them in it.'

Capella had spoken with a perverse pride in the ruthlessness of the local mafia. He was, Alvarez thought, justified. Mallorca might be the Island of Calm, but those on the wrong side of the law could be every bit as vicious as anyone from the toughest of inner cities. Further, the community was relatively small and tightly knit and its members enjoyed the peasant's ability to notice events so apparently insignificant that another would miss them, while even those who were completely law abiding—Mallorquin style—suffered from xenophobia which had merely been put on hold by tourist money.

Yet to assume that Clough was not in drugs was to promote unwanted questions. Why had Lewis come to the island unless to collect money from Clough? Why had Clough given him—assuming he had—a million pesetas? How had Sheard, who had not previously known Lewis, quickly become so involved in whatever was going on that he had had to be murdered? . . . Or were all these questions false because the supposition on which each was based was fallacious?

Capella again banged his empty glass down on the table. Another small brandy might just help him to sort out his own muddled mind, Alvarez decided.

*   *   *

Thursday was hotter and more airless than ever. Although it was early, the thought of an iced drink before the meal was an irresistible one. Alvarez left the office. The old square was filled with tourists who had nothing better to do than idle their day away. He looked at them with the resentment of envy, unlocked his car to find the interior was an oven because he had forgotten to leave the windows slightly open. Some became martyrs to their duty.

As he stepped into the house, the phone began to ring. He lifted the receiver.

'It's the lab here. I tried to phone you at your office, but there was no answer; they said you might be at home and gave me your number. We have the results of the analyses and I thought you'd like to hear them. Negative.'

'How d'you mean?'

'Pure Scotch in the one bottle, the hint of pure Scotch in the other bottle and the glasses.'

'But . . . but that's impossible!'

'The impossible happens with regular monotony here.'

'I was certain there was some sort of narcotic in the whisky.'

'You could drink the bottle and not suffer anything but the usual hangover.'

He thanked the caller for ringing, stared unseeingly at a framed print of a stylized Mallorquin country setting. If one built a house of paper, one should not be surprised if it was blown down. If Lewis had not been drugged, the probability had to be that he had not been murdered, but *had* been so tight when he fell over the side he'd been unable to swim; Clough's wife *had* spent a million pesetas on two dresses; Lewis *had* tapped a source of money that had nothing to do with Clough; it *was* one more coincidence that Lewis had mentioned the name 'Larry' to Cara; it *was* yet another coincidence that Sheard had been on one of the two routes to Annuig when he'd died in a fatal crash and Traffic's theory of events was wrong ... Like disasters, coincidences often did not come singly ...

He wandered through to the dining/sitting-room. Isabel and Juan were arguing and Jaime was seated at the table, bottle and glass in front of him.

Isabel looked up. 'Uncle, where's Valparaiso?'

'Argentina, silly,' said Juan, with condescending superiority.

'It isn't.'

'You don't know anything.'

'I know more than you.'

Dolores pushed her way through the bead curtain. 'What's all the noise about?'

Knowing how sharp she could be, they were

silent, each waiting for the other to answer and thereby suffer the brunt of her annoyance.

'Well?'

Isabel's indignation overcame her sense of caution. 'He says Valparaiso is in Argentina.'

'It's in Chile. Juan, you should know your geography better than that.'

'I was just pulling her leg.'

'Then do it more peacefully.' She returned to the kitchen.

Jaime leaned across the table and spoke to Alvarez in a low voice. 'Instead of giving them hell, she just asks them to be more peaceful; she saw the bottle of brandy, but didn't have a go at me for drinking too much—I tell you, it's worrying me sick, her being so reasonable.' He picked up the bottle and refilled his glass.

Alvarez had too many troubles of his own to give much thought to Jaime's.

*　　*　　*

He parked, walked along to the Hotel Alhambra. The younger receptionist said that Señorita Glass had left—obviously for the beach—roughly an hour before.

Alvarez returned to his car, drove to the front and searched for a parking space; since the local council had reduced the number of them for reasons which escaped anyone who relied on common sense, he ended by parking on a yellow line. He walked along until level with the point at which Kirsty would have reached the beach had she made directly for it and stepped on to the sand. As he searched for her amongst the dozens of sunbathers, he could not escape the bitter truth: age condemned. The young could display their bodies with happy conclusions, the older with only unhappy self-delusions.

Kirsty was young and therefore it was a pleasure—solely from an artistic point of view—to see her topless. He was sorry that she was in the company of a bronzed, slicked-down beach leech.

'Good afternoon, señorita,' he said as he came to a stop.

The young man looked up, shielding his eyes with his hand. 'You want?' he asked in heavily accented, drawling English.

'To speak to the señorita,' Alvarez replied, also in English.

'Some different time, man. Blow.'

'Carlos, he's . . .' Kirsty began hurriedly.

He interrupted her. 'An old man. He troubles more, I blow away.'

'Don't blow too hard,' Alvarez said roughly in Mallorquin, bitter at the description of himself, 'or you'll end up very short of breath.'

'Who are you?'

'Cuerpo General de Policia.'

The young man tried to maintain a cocky air, but his tone was far less aggressive when he said: 'What d'you want?'

98

'To speak to the señorita. So it is up to you to blow.'

'I was just going.' He stood, brushed sand off his chest. 'I be with you later,' he said to Kirsty, before walking off with as much strutting pride as he could muster.

Alvarez sat on the sand and was careful not to look too openly at her shapely breasts.

'I met Carlos yesterday...' She became silent. She looked at him, then away. 'I liked Bert a lot, I really did, and it was terrible what happened. Only, as Cara keeps saying, it's no good going on and on being miserable as we're on holiday. We've only three days left.'

'Then I trust they are happier than those which have gone before.'

She scooped up some sand, let it trickle through her fingers. 'Has ... has something more happened?'

'No.'

'Then why...?'

'I want to talk to you again about the night you were on the boat.'

'Must you? I mean ...'

'Yes, señorita?'

'I've been trying so hard to forget.'

And with the help of Carlos, succeeding. She looked so young and—if the word still had any meaning—innocent, that the degree of her amorality shocked as well as surprised him. 'I will be as brief as possible. You have told me it was Señor Lewis who opened the full bottle of whisky. By then, had Señorita Fenn had too much to drink?'

'I've told you, no one had.'

'Can you be so very certain?'

'When Cara's had a skinful, she gets all giggly and mixes up her words. She wasn't like that at all.'

'Señor Lewis poured a drink for each of you?'

'Yeah, even though l said I didn't want one.'

'Señor Sheard began to yawn and complain of dizziness. Were Señorita Fenn and Señor Lewis also showing signs of tiredness and dizziness?'

She leaned forward until her breasts were pressing against her raised legs, wrapped her arms around her legs and interlaced her fingers, rested her chin on one knee and watched a waterskier criss-cross the wake of a towing speedboat. 'I don't know, I mean, I wasn't thinking about what they were doing.'

'But perhaps you noticed them just briefly before you fell asleep?'

'They was both flat out. Asleep, I mean. And I can remember thinking that the way Cara was lying, if she wasn't careful she'd end up on the floor. Which is what she did.'

The course of events suggested the full bottle of whisky had been drugged; the forensic evidence made it certain it had not been. 'During the night, you seemed to hear someone moving about the cabin?'

'It was a nightmare.'

'The last time we spoke about it, you weren't all that certain it was.'

'Well, I am now.'

She found it far preferable to believe her memory to be the product of a nightmare than to live with the possibility that she had heard Lewis's moving aft so that, if she'd pulled herself together, she might have saved him after he'd fallen overboard. 'Can you describe what kind of movements they were?'

'Nothing's normal in a nightmare.'

He was not going to learn from her any facts that would confirm or deny the possibility that she had half heard—being less deeply drugged than the others—someone's exchanging both whisky and glasses in order to hide evidence which would have shown Lewis had been murdered. He stood. 'Thank you, señorita, for kindly recalling times you so wish to forget. I shall not be troubling you again.'

She unwrapped her arms and lay back, propping herself up on her elbows.

Her movement had, through no conscious volition on his part, caused him to shift his gaze. Her breasts were more silken and shapely than a ripe persimmon . . .

As he walked across the sand towards the pine trees, he wondered who was the fool who had first dubbed women the weaker sex.

CHAPTER TWELVE

Alvarez sat by a window in the Club Llueso and drank the last of the coffee and brandy. Today was Friday, tomorrow was Saturday. Only in very unusual circumstances did he have to work on Saturday afternoons. The day after was Sunday. Circumstances had to be quite exceptional for him to have to work on a Sunday. And to add to such a rosy future, Dolores's mood remained so sunny that lunch must surely be another feast.

He looked at his watch and was surprised to discover how long he'd been in the club. He paid the bill and walked across the square, then down the road to the post. He had been seated at his desk for less than a minute, contemplating the confusion of papers, files, unopened letters, memoranda, and notes to himself which didn't make sense, when the phone rang. The plum-voiced secretary told him that the superior chief wished to speak to him. No day could be perfect, he thought philosophically.

'Have you received the report in the Lewis case from the Laboratory of Forensic Sciences?' Salas demanded.

'The preliminary one, yes, señor.'

'Then you'll know that it makes clear that neither the whisky in the bottle, nor the dregs in the second bottle or the glasses contained any form of narcotic?'

'That is so, señor.'

'Thus there is now no logical reason to doubt that the missing man's disappearance was the result of a drunken accident?'

'When there are circumstances which seem to be ambiguous . . .'

'It is you, Alvarez, who delights in adding ambiguity to every circumstance. If confusion is not already present, you rush to introduce it.'

'Yet in this case . . .'

'There can now be no confusion.'

'I'm still perplexed by . . .'

'By virtually everything. The head of the laboratory has informed me of the total bill he will be presenting to the department. Have you any idea how large it is?'

'I'm afraid not, señor.'

'Well over two hundred and fifty thousand pesetas.'

'That seems rather a lot . . .'

'When one remembers that the analyses were not authorized, it is a very large sum indeed.'

'As I explained, it was my opinion that in the circumstances it was essential for the tests to be carried out to discover if the whisky had been drugged.'

'What circumstances?'

'The fact that they all fell asleep on the job.'

'What job?'

'Sex, señor.'

'My God! Are you under some perverse compulsion? Do you have to introduce the subject into every conversation?'

Alvarez said hurriedly: 'Then there was Señorita Glass's nightmare . . .'

'Are you now saying that the basis for your investigation has been a woman's nightmare? Then, no doubt, you have also consulted a clairvoyant and a necromancer?'

'The thing is, I thought that . . .'

'I have neither the time nor the inclination to follow the course of your thoughts. In future, you will exactly observe each and every rule of procedure, with no exceptions. Is that clear?'

'Yes, señor.'

'There is no room for confusion?'

'No, señor.'

The line went dead.

Alvarez replaced the receiver. The superior chief was, perhaps, confused about the nature of Kirsty's nightmare.

*　　　*　　　*

Pascoe had made a fortune from the production of pornographic videos. But since the expatriate community tended to be small-minded, he always claimed he'd been in educational publishing.

Naturally, a man of his position needed to own a boat even when he feared the sea and he had been on the point of buying a forty-foot motor cruiser when, just in time, he'd learned that an acquaintance had ordered a forty-two footer; he had immediately changed his purchase to a forty-five footer. He was a gregarious man and enjoyed entertaining lavishly, especially aboard his cruiser, especially those who had cause to envy him.

When under way, he liked to be on the flying bridge, wearing a peak cap with scrambled egg, tilted at a nautical angle. He employed Milne full-time as pilot, deckhand, engineer, greaser, and steward.

Milne, at the wheel, said: 'Will this do you, Cap'n?'

It had never occurred to him to wonder whether 'Cap'n' was touched with sarcasm rather than respect. He visually searched the sea. The island was some five kilometres to the north, most of its details scrambled by the heat haze; between it and them were two yachts, ghosting along in the lightest of breezes. He considered yachtspeople the greatest of bores, preferring to talk of sheets, halyards, tacks and greybeards, rather than indexes, futures, scrip issues, and P/E rates. On the port beam was a ship, hull down. 'Stop engines.'

Milne reached forward to bring both engine control joy-sticks back to neutral, then switched off. The faint noise of the boat's movements and the water gently slapping against her hull became audible.

'Keep a good lookout,' Pascoe ordered.

'Aye, aye, Cap'n.'

He adjusted the rake of his cap, made his way down the companionway and into the saloon, then aft to the open deck where a tarpaulin had been rigged to give shade. Several men and women were gathered, drinking with the enthusiasm of poor relations.

'Must be eight bells,' Kerr said.

'How d'you mean?'

'The end of the watch.'

Pascoe was annoyed by his failure to understand. 'I've decided we'll lie idle for a bit,' he said pompously. He disliked Kerr, who was more or less permanently drunk and also one of *them* however, his brother was a noted landowner in Scotland. He moved to the centre of the deck, braced his feet against a nonexistent swell, cupped his hands about his mouth to overcome a nonexistent gale, and called out: 'Who's for a swim before lunch?'

Monica, over made-up, under-dressed, her decolletage only just giving imagination work to do, said in her husky voice; 'I didn't think we'd be swimming. I haven't brought a costume.'

Turner could be relied upon to make the obvious comment. 'Then go in skinny.'

She fluttered her eyelashes. 'And have you ogling me?'

'I promise not to look.'

'My mother told me never to believe a man's promise unless he's got his legs crossed.'

'Very wise,' said Hilda Pascoe. Plump, cheerful, content with whatever life offered, she regretted her husband's thrusting social ambitions since it meant she had so often to mix with people she would rather not have done. 'And there's no call for anyone to get excited because we've several costumes in the cabins and I'm sure one of them will fit you nicely.'

'That's what I call optimism,' Turner said.

Hilda and Monica went into the saloon and for'd to the cabins, others followed. Within five minutes, most were in the water.

It was Turner, a couple of hundred metres from the boat, who suddenly began to shout and to wave his arms. The other swimmers, unable to see him clearly, if at all, assumed he was fooling and someone called out to enquire whether he had been foul-hooked by Monica. Milne, however, up on the flying bridge and able to look down and judge the sense of panic in Turner's movements, grabbed a pair of binoculars and looked through them. It was immediately clear that Turner had not been attacked by cramp because he had begun to swim back to the boat with a stylish crawl. Milne visually searched the surrounding sea, remembering the authenticated stories of great white sharks in the Mediterranean; he made ready to start the motors, accepting that should this be a shark attack, he'd never get the boat under way in time. He picked out something

107

that floated so close to the surface that from time to time parts of it broke through to become clearly visible. For a while he could not identify what it was; when he did, he swore.

*   *   *

Few moments were filled with such blissful satisfaction as when, on a boiling Saturday afternoon, having dined and wined to perfection, and taken a little more brandy as a digestif, one retired to the bedroom, stripped off and lay down on the bed, knowing one did not have to return to the office, shut one's eyes and allowed one's mind to go walkabout. Image drifted into image, each becoming that little more abstract . . .

Downstairs, the phone rang.

Jerked awake, Alvarez cursed the caller with all the crude viciousness of which Mallorquin was capable. As the ringing continued, he wondered why Dolores was not hurrying downstairs. Should he stir himself to go along the corridor and hammer on her bedroom door to alert her . . . The ringing ceased.

He reached across to adjust the fan slightly so that the draught of air struck higher up his side, snuggled his head down on the pillow. He was just about to fall asleep when the phone rang again. Clearly, after it had automatically disconnected because the call had not been answered, the fool at the other end had dialled again . . .

Footsteps passed his door. Dolores had at last decided to go down. He hoped she would, despite her present sunny humour, tell the caller what she thought of someone who rang during the siesta . . .

The bang on the door was so unexpected—he had not heard her return upstairs—that he started. 'It's for you,' she called out.

'Are you sure?'

There was no answer.

Reluctantly, he sat up, swivelled round, stood, put on his trousers—she insisted that no member of the house walked around in underclothes—and went downstairs.

'It's the post . . .'

He interrupted the speaker. 'What's the idea of phoning at this time of the afternoon?'

'Have to do my duty, you lazy bastard.'

'It's Agustin, isn't it? I'll see you get a conduct report that has you spending the next ten years in some godforsaken village in the centre of Andalucia.'

'You reckon the teniente will listen to anything you have to say? . . . The port's just been through. A motor cruiser's come into harbour to say they've sighted a body floating five kilometres off the bay.'

'So?'

'So they marked it with a buoy and now you can go out and help recover it.'

'My job can't start until the body's landed.'

'If they made a mistake and dropped you off at the pearly gates, you'd wait for St Peter to open 'em.'

'Each man to a job; each job to a man.'

*   *   *

The open fishing boat, built to traditional design, approached the curving shore midway between the port and the small, ugly holiday village—a point of the bay where there was the least likelihood of there being any tourists. The helmsman put the single-cylinder diesel into neutral, then reverse, to cut the boat's way and prevent her running her bows on to the shingle. Two cabos, trousers rolled up, cursing everything and everybody, waded out, lifted up a body-bag and carried it ashore.

If there were anything Alvarez disliked more than looking at death, he could not readily name it; to look at it was to see the image of one's own precarious mortality, to be reminded that even that brief prick of pain as one had climbed out of bed could be the first call to join the victim. Mentally bracing himself, he pulled back the edge of the bag until he could gain a clear view of the face. Death was often described as merciful; its aftermath never was. He recognized Lewis from the passport photograph, but it required a considerable degree of imaginative reconstruction to do so.

CHAPTER THIRTEEN

On the Tuesday, Alvarez returned to the post to be informed by the duty cabo that the Institute of Forensic Anatomy had telephoned and wanted him to call back. He went up the stairs, into his office, and sat. After he'd regained his breath, he dialled Palma.

'The cause of death was drowning,' said Professor Fortunato's assistant. 'There can be no doubt about that with all the classical signs present—ballooning of the lungs, marked congestion and cyanosis in the right side of the heart, microscopic diatomaceous matter in the air passages and stomach. That he drowned in salt water is evidenced by the fact that the chloride content in the left heart is higher than in the right. But we do have a query as to whether he suffered an assault before death.'

Alvarez drew in his breath sharply. 'How strong a query?'

'There's the rub. The temperature of the sea has meant decomposition has taken place quite quickly and there's been considerable damage from fish. If you'd like the details . . .'

'Thank you, just the conclusions,' he replied quickly.

'There are two lines of bruising on the back. Unfortunately, we cannot determine whether these were caused before or immediately after death. As you know, floating debris often batters bodies in the sea through wave or wind action and this is probably the most likely explanation. However, there is one interesting thing about the bruising—the lines are parallel, some thirty centimetres apart. It calls for quite a coincidence for two objects floating in the water to strike the body either at the same or different times at angles parallel to each other.

'On the other hand, it's difficult to envisage an offensive weapon that consists of two bars thirty centimetres apart—very clumsy. Of course, there remains the possibility that two separate blows were struck by an attacker, but that recalls the problem of the bruises being parallel. Could be a coincidence; they do happen.'

With disconcerting frequency. 'Assume these bruises were caused by a blow, would they have knocked Lewis to the ground?'

'Hard to answer. The best I can offer is that he would at least have had a job to keep his balance.'

'Would they have incapacitated him?'

'I doubt it. That is, unless in falling he suffered further damage.'

'There's no evidence of any?'

'None.'

'In a nutshell, you can't say with any certainty what did happen?'

'I'm afraid not. Sorry about that, but the state of the body makes it impossible. After several days in the water at the height of summer . . .'

'It's anybody's guess,' Alvarez cut in, wondering again why pathologists seemed always so keen to pass on the grislier details of their work. He thanked the other, rang off. He scratched the side of his nose as he stared through the window at the blank wall of the building on the opposite side of the road. On its own, the evidence he had just been given was as ambiguous as previous evidence. But if he could show that even one part of it was unambiguous . . .

He drove down to the port, parked, and went into the office of Gomila y Hijos. The young woman was again painting her nails and she again viewed him with disdain, plainly not remembering who he was. He reminded her.

'What is it this time?' she asked.

'Is the *Aventura* still in port?'

She shrugged her shoulders.

'Perhaps you could be very kind and stop work long enough to check,' he said with sarcastic politeness.

Sullenly, she tapped out instructions on the keyboard and the information came up on the VDU. 'No one has chartered it, so it must be here.'

'A boat is always feminine.'

'Because it's beautiful,' she said, and giggled.

Although the distance was so short, he drove to the eastern arm of the harbour and parked

113

as near to the *Aventura as* he could go. In such heat, unnecessary exercise was dangerous.

He had forgotten the gangplank. He swallowed repeatedly, called on St Christopher, and finally, eyes firmly fixed high above the yawning hell beneath him and despite the terrible, perverse temptation to look down, boarded.

He used a metal tape measure to determine the gap between rails at the stern. Thirty-one centimetres. So here was the coincidence too many. He pictured the murderer climbing aboard as the *Aventura* lay at anchor, entering the cabin where the four lay drugged, grabbing Lewis and dragging him out of the saloon— half-heard by Kirsty—and struggling to bundle him over the stern. An uncoordinated body was one of the most difficult things to handle, with arms and legs flopping this way and that and unexpectedly altering the centre of balance. As he'd tried to heave the unconscious Lewis over the rails, he had lost control and Lewis's back had slammed into them. In the water, the murderer had held the body underneath . . .

Alvarez replaced the tape measure in his pocket. For once, Salas was going to have to admit his work had been inspired and faultless.

*   *   *

He phoned Palma at a quarter to six that evening and spoke to Salas's secretary. 'May I
114

speak to the superior chief?'

'No,' she replied.

'It is important.'

'It doesn't matter. He's had to fly to Salamanca.'

'When will he be back?'

'I have no idea.'

'Can you get in touch with him?'

'If you want something, you'll have to speak to Comisario Borne.'

He thanked her, rang off.

Comisario Borne was a man who took life so seriously that he believed his superiors' edicts were engraved on tablets of stone; who lacked the imagination to see how a fact might suggest one thing taken on its own, but could point to something entirely different when slotted in with another fact. It would be useless to ask Comisario Borne to override an order of the superior chief. Yet to conduct any further investigation into the deaths of Lewis and Sheard before he had express permission to do so would be asking for trouble . . .

He left the building and returned to his car, drove out of Llueso, through the Laraix valley and up the twisting, tortuous road to the mountains. He parked in a natural lay-by, left the car and crossed to the shade of an evergreen oak where he sat on a rounded boulder. To his left was a valley, on the far side of which the mountain slopes were bare except for odd patches of scrub grass; to his right, the uneven land, pitted with outcrops of rock striated by age and patched with clumps of bowed trees, rose to become the flanks of more mountains which were higher, starker, and touched with menace even in the harsh sunshine. There was not a building in sight.

He came here when he was troubled. The solitude, the land that had not altered in aeons and was therefore both past and present, the acceptance of the fact that amidst such natural grandeur he was an alien, produced in his mind a feeling of total insignificance; experience had taught him that only when one knew that one was totally insignificant did one begin to think with true honesty.

When he was convinced that he was right and everyone else was wrong, was his conviction fuelled by perverse pride? Salas thought him incompetent, so did he contradict merely because this was a weak man's way of trying to assert himself? Born a peasant, had he remained a stubborn, bloody-minded peasant?

He believed justice to be only slightly less essential to a man than the food he ate, the water he drank, and the air he breathed. Without justice, there could only be chaos in which the few strong prospered and the many weak perished. Justice demanded the truth, so surely if a man sought it he must be in the right, even if his motive for doing so might be suspect?

He drove back to the village, went up to his

116

office, phoned the Institute of Forensic Anatomy and asked for a full analysis of Lewis's blood to be made.

He replaced the receiver. It was mortifying to realize how long it had taken him to work out that if someone had doped the whisky, had waited until it had taken effect, then swum to the boat and dragged Lewis over the side and drowned him, that someone was a man of imagination and forethought; such a man would replace the doped bottle of whisky and the glasses so that if any suspicion was raised and an analysis of their contents carried out, the result would be negative, leading to the conclusion that Lewis's death had been an accident.

*   *   *

The two calls came in quick succession on Thursday morning.

'We've completed our analysis in the Lewis case,' said the assistant at the Forensic Institute of Anatomy.

'Have you found anything?'

'We have.'

Alvarez enjoyed the narcissistic satisfaction of having proved the world wrong.

'Are you familiar with chloral hydrate?'

'I don't think so.'

'It's a hypnotic, occasionally used medicinally to induce a condition resembling

117

natural sleep. In the past, it was a favourite with criminals who encouraged potential victims to drink something into which it had been introduced; then the victims could be robbed at no risk to themselves.'

'You're talking about a Mickey Finn! I didn't recognize it by its proper name. So that's how Lewis was drugged!'

'To be precise, no. Chloral hydrate is usually described as having a disagreeable taste—you or I would call it filthy. So it was difficult to obscure this in a drink and if the intended victim wasn't more than half seas over, he'd probably take one mouthful and spit it out. But a renegade chemist in the States who'd been working on the problem managed to eliminate most of the foul taste with a slight modification in the hydrolysis of the trichloroethanal. As a result, the narcotic could be introduced into a dry martini or a bloody Mary and, even if sober, the victim would cheerfully drink it. According to reports, this modified narcotic has only one drawback in so far as the criminal is concerned. It promotes a temporary hysterical violence in a few people before they pass out. One would-be thief was beaten to a bloody pulp before his victim collapsed. A rare case of the biter being bit!'

'And it was this modified chloral hydrate that Lewis drank?'

'It was.'

As soon as the call was finished, Alvarez

reached down to open the bottom right-hand drawer of the desk and bring out a bottle of brandy and a glass. He was about to pour himself a congratulatory drink when the phone rang again.

'Are you really as stupid as your actions inevitably suggest?' demanded Salas.

'I understood you were in Salamanca, señor . . .'

'Did I, or did I not, order you to close inquiries into the death of the Englishman, Lewis?'

'Yes, but . . .'

'One more "but" and you join the ranks of the unemployed. Did you, or did you not, agree that my order was incapable of misinterpretation?'

'Yes, señor, only . . .'

'Only instead of misinterpreting it, you flatly disobeyed it by asking the Institute to carry out further analyses of specimens from the dead man.'

'Because of the facts . . .'

'Which informed you—or would have done, were you capable of accepting information—that there was no evidence to suggest the cause of death had been anything but accidental drowning.'

'Actually, there were two bruises on the dead man's back . . .'

'Which you were told could well have been caused after death.'

119

'The thing is, they were parallel and thirty centimetres apart.'

'Had they been twenty or forty, you would have accepted the obvious conclusion without argument?'

'That made me think.'

'Please do not exaggerate.'

'I went aboard the *Aventura* and measured the distance between the rails at the stern. They are thirty-one centimetres middle to middle. This makes it almost certain that the bruises were caused when Lewis fell against them.'

'It has not occurred to you that a drunken man tends to fall about?'

'All the evidence suggests he wasn't drunk.'

'Evidence provided by equally sottish companions.'

'I'm sure Señorita Glass wasn't tight. She has a rather delicate stomach and if she drinks very much, she suffers . . .'

'How is it that when you are asked to explain your total disregard of orders, you start talking about some woman's digestive problems?'

'I was trying to explain why I'm certain Lewis wasn't drunk.'

'If he was sober when he fell, he'd have swum back and pulled himself aboard; if for some reason he couldn't do that, he would have called for help.'

'He didn't fall overboard, señor.'

'Have you taken complete leave of your

senses? Haven't you been trying to tell me that the bruises on his back were caused when he fell overboard?'

'When he fell against the rails. He was dragged out of the saloon and thrown over the stern. But it's very difficult to manage an unconscious body and as he was heaved over, his body jackknifed and his back hit the rails with considerable force.'

'You are now suggesting that one of the others on the boat, who according to you only a moment ago were all unconscious, threw him over the side?'

'The murderer swam out from the shore or, more likely, another boat . . .'

'Why content yourself with but one aquatic homicidal maniac? Why not take the chance to compound confusion by suggesting two, three, four? . . . You should not be surprised to learn I consider that this conversation has confirmed the proposition that you are not fit to hold the position you do. It is therefore my intention . . .'

'Señor.'

'Don't interrupt.'

'Have you spoken to the Institute of Forensic Anatomy?'

'How else did I learn that you had flatly disobeyed my orders; that when informed there was every reason to suppose the drowning was accidental, your immediate reaction was to ask for full and very costly analyses to be made of specimens from the dead man?'

'But they didn't give you the results?'

'Hardly necessary.'

'They phoned me just before you did. Lewis had been drugged with modified chloral hydrate, which explains why he didn't cry out or swim.'

There was a long pause. 'What is chloral hydrate?'

'We know it as a Mickey Finn. Apparently it used to be so foul-tasting it was difficult to disguise even in a strong drink, but a chemist in America has managed to make it much less obnoxious so that now it's all too easy to use successfully. It has only one unpredictable disadvantage . . .'

'There can be no doubt?'

'None, señor.' Alvarez thought that a little joke might lessen the superior chief's resentment. 'I reckon we ought to christen the new dope, Mickey Swede.'

Salas cut the connection.

Alvarez poured himself a larger drink than he would have done had the superior chief not phoned.

CHAPTER FOURTEEN

The fax from England arrived on Friday morning; it proved to be a fuller report than

Alvarez had expected.

Lawrence Charles Clough had no criminal record and his name was not on the 'yellow list'. (There was no explanation of this term, but it was obvious that it referred to the information all detective forces collected and kept on file— the names of men and women suspected of crimes for which there was insufficient evidence to bring any charges.) He had been engaged in property development and had run into trouble with investments which had become of doubtful value due to the general economic malaise. The banks from whom he'd borrowed capital, watching the fall in property prices, had demanded either repayment or further security. He had sought and found the latter by marrying Vera Reece, a very wealthy woman; she had allowed a part of her fortune to be used as security against his debts. At a later date, he had identified some land which was for sale and which he believed could restore his fortunes. She had agreed with the bankers to increase the amount of her capital being used as security, but only days later had cancelled this agreement; then, the following week, she had renewed her pledge. The reason for this was not known, but it did seem reasonable to assume that she had suspected her husband of being unfaithful (he was known not to take his marriage vows seriously), but he had somehow convinced her that she was wrong. Earlier this year, he had managed to gain planning permission for the land in question and with the proceeds gained from selling it, he had been able to liquidate his debts. Not long after this, he and his wife had left England to live abroad.

Little was known about Neil Andrew Lewis, prior to his conviction for robbery at the age of nineteen. At the age of twenty-three, he had been convicted along with two other men of robbery with violence and had served four and a half years before being released from prison towards the end of the previous year.

Neither man had any known connection with the drug trade.

Alvarez put the fax down on his desk. If not drugs, what? Blackmail?

*   *   *

He rounded a bend to come in sight of Son Preda. Envy might be one of the deadly sins, but how was one to avoid it when looking at such an estate? Were he to win El Gordo, or the primitiva when the bote had risen to eight hundred million, he'd buy such a place and lavish his newly-won money on the land. The olive trees would be pruned and harvested; the olive press would be restored and the olives, packed in layers and squeezed by the huge wooden press driven by a mule, would give up their golden-green virgin oil. The water wheels would be restored so that their leather buckets dipped down to scoop up water, then rose to discharge it into channels that led to the estanques. There would be no diesel-stinking tractors, compacting the earth, no combines designed for prairie vastness, dodging around almond and fig trees and breaking their branches; only mules and horses, single furrow Roman ploughs, reapers and binders, and the corn would be winnowed by the wind as it had been until only a few years ago . . .

He sighed. There was no fool more senseless than the one who looked to the past instead of the future.

He braked to a halt in front of the house, climbed out of the car, crossed to the stone steps and climbed these, swung the heavy wrought-iron knocker to cause the deep, thudding sound that came from the past he so espoused.

The door was opened by a young woman in maid's uniform whom he'd not previously met. 'Is the señor in?' he asked.

Her manner was direct, rather than diplomatic. 'Why d'you want to know?'

'Inspector Alvarez, Cuerpo General de Policia.'

She looked at him with some interest, but remained unimpressed. 'He's been out since just after breakfast.'

'Then is the señora in?'

'As far as I know.'

'I'd like a word with her.'

'Then you'd best come in.'

She led him into the same room as before. After she'd gone, he studied the flintlock rifles. Who was most at risk when one of these was fired—the man in front or the man behind?

He heard the door open and turned. As Vera Clough entered, he said: 'Good morning, senora. I hope I am not unduly disturbing you.'

'I'm afraid my husband's out.'

'So the maid told me.' Once again, he was vaguely surprised by her appearance—the rich usually, subtly or unsubtly, flaunted their wealth, but she made no effort to do so. 'I need to speak to you as well as to your husband.'

'I . . .' She hesitated, then spoke in a rush. 'I think he ought to be here.'

'Naturally I will wait if you wish. But I've only come to give you some serious news and ask you to confirm what you have previously told me.'

'What serious news?'

'You will remember that when last here I asked if you or your husband knew Señor Lewis who had disappeared from a boat and had to be presumed drowned. Very sadly, that presumption has been confirmed. Further, we can now be certain that his death was not an accident and he was murdered.'

'Oh, my God!' She gesticulated with her hands. 'It's impossible.'

'Why is that?'

'Because . . .' She took a couple of paces to

126

her right, slumped down in a chair.

He patiently waited.

'My husband told you how this sort of thing affects me,' she said in a low voice, staring at the floor.

'Indeed, señora, which is why I so regret having had to tell you.' Her reaction to the news had been far stronger than he would have expected, even allowing for her emotional identification with others' miseries. 'I will be as brief as possible.' And also as quick as possible, hoping that that would prevent her remembering to demand that her husband be present. 'Are you positive you have never met Señor Lewis?'

'Of course I am.'

'And he's never been in contact with you either by phone or letter?'

'No.'

'So he has not attempted to blackmail you or your husband?' He noticed that she suddenly clasped her hands together on her lap; she had acted similarly when she'd first learned of Lewis's death. People often unknowingly betrayed an inner tension.

'Of course he hasn't,' she said loudly.

'If he had, it would be in your interests to admit that fact.'

'It's a ridiculous thing to suggest.'

'Señora, these days, when little or nothing in a person's private life is considered sufficiently immoral to be concealed at all costs, blackmail is levied almost always on someone who has committed a serious criminal act. The police, knowing that the victim's evidence will be necessary to prosecute the blackmailer successfully, treat that crime as sympathetically as is possible.'

'He wasn't blackmailing us.'

'I'm sorry that it's been my job to suggest such a possibility . . . There is one final thing. May I see the frocks, please?'

'What frocks?' She stared at him, panicking because she could not understand the question and therefore fearing it the more.

'The ones you had made by the lady from England who, understandably, has no wish to pay taxes.'

She tightened the grip of her hands. 'I . . . You'll have to ask my husband about them.'

He stood. 'Thank you very much for your help, señora.'

As he drove along the dirt track towards the road, he thought that luck had finally been with him. Because Clough had not been there to act as a shield, his wife had surely confirmed the motive for Lewis's murder.

Alvarez braked to a halt, checked there was no oncoming traffic, turned on to the road. Lewis had been blackmailing her, her husband, or both of them. So what had Lewis known that was so dangerous to them that it had been worthwhile paying him a million pesetas to buy his temporary silence, then to kill him to ensure

128

this became permanent; later, to kill Sheard, who must have learned enough to be in a position to have continued the blackmail?

Was he right to judge from her reactions that she had had no reason to believe Lewis had been murdered?

*　　*　　*

Dolores had just served the sopes Mallorquines when the phone rang. She did not ask if the two men were deaf, but immediately moved her chair back from the table and left. Jaime watched her, a look of worry on his face.

When she returned, she said: 'It's the post.'

'Don't they ever relax,' Alvarez muttered with annoyance. He helped himself to another spoonful of the soup—more a stew, with cabbage, tomatoes, garlic, onions, olive oil, seasoning, and brown sopes bread—and went through to the phone.

'I've had a foreigner ringing in. Couldn't understand a word, so in the end he got his maid to talk. She said he wanted to speak to you and it wouldn't be to tell you what a nice guy you are. I told her that being a lazy bastard, you were at home, guzzling. The next thing, he's demanding your home number. I refused. When would you be back at work? Just before it was time to pack up for the day and go home, I told her . . . So this is just to warn you that he'll be ringing in some time and, from the sound of things, you'll need to brace yourself.'

'Thanks for the warning.'

'My old woman always says my good nature makes a fool of me.'

It was only after replacing the receiver that Alvarez realized the duty cabo had failed to name the caller. Still, that had been unnecessary. Clough, accepting that the best defence was attack, had made his first move.

He returned to the dining-room.

'Is it trouble?' Dolores asked solicitously.

'Work's always trouble,' he answered as he refilled his glass with wine.

*   *   *

The expected phone call was made at half past six.

'Would you be kind enough to tell me exactly what is going on, Inspector?'

The degree of a Mallorquin's temper could be gauged by the range and explosiveness of his expletives, but an Englishman often offered no guide other than the increased iciness of his politeness.

'If you are referring to my visit this morning to your home, as I explained to the senora, it has been established that Señor Lewis was murdered. It has therefore become necessary to conduct a more detailed and even more urgent investigation.'

'That is supposed to be an explanation for

accusing my wife of being a criminal?'

'I certainly did not do that.'

'You asked if either of us had been subjected to blackmail and then went on to say that these days it almost always follows a crime which has been committed by the person blackmailed. You would not agree that the inference is quite unmistakable?'

'What I was trying to do was not to accuse the senora of anything, but merely to assure her that had either of you been subjected to blackmail at the hands of Lewis, it would be very much in your interests to admit that fact because authority will always offer as much sympathy as is possible ... I am afraid it is sometimes very difficult to express oneself accurately in a foreign language.'

'Your sole aim was to be helpful?'

'Indeed, señor.'

'Then would you care to explain why you thought such help to be necessary?'

Which question, Alvarez thought, brought them back to the beginning.

'Inspector, I was under the impression that when you were here several days ago I fully answered all the points you raised—and answered them to your satisfaction. Yet it seems, to put it bluntly, that you believe me to have been lying.'

'That is not so.'

'If you believed me, you would not have bothered to explain to my wife the benefits of admitting to a criminal action and then to ask to see the two dresses which had been made for her.'

'Señor, you are overlooking something. When I first spoke to you and the señora, Señor Lewis was missing and I was trying to establish whether he was, in fact, dead. Now that I know he was murdered, I have to conduct a much more detailed investigation and that means it becomes necessary to re-examine some of the earlier evidence.'

'It perhaps has not occurred to you that a man in my position is unlikely to have given anyone cause for blackmail?'

'Señor, surely the quickest and simplest way of clearing up any misunderstanding is to give me the name and address of the lady who made your wife's dresses? The moment she confirms all you have told me, there can be no question that you gave the million pesetas to Lewis.'

'I explained why I'm not prepared to do that.'

'The circumstances now are very different.'

'However changed, they cannot concern me. I gave my word to the lady.'

What did one call a man who claimed to place honour above self-preservation? A hypocrite or a dinosaur?

'While naturally willing to do all I can to assist, that does not mean I am prepared meekly to suffer harassment. I hope this is clear?'

'Yes, señor.'

He said a polite goodbye, rang off.

Alvarez settled back in his chair. However smart he might once have been in the business world, Clough had just shown he was ham-fisted outside it. Believing he was dealing with a slow-witted peasant who would bow to a show of authority, he had set out to choke off any further investigation. Had he understood the peasant mentality, he would have known that even while bowing, the peasant was mentally sticking up two fingers.

How to take the investigation forward, when there were so few facts, so much supposition? . . . Before he had come to the island, Lewis had been on the Peninsula. Obviously, he'd been in funds. Money he had been paid for carrying out the criminal act, the commission of which had placed him in a position to blackmail Clough? In the top pocket of Lewis's jacket hanging in the hotel cupboard had been a used rail ticket from Bitges to Barcelona . . .

CHAPTER FIFTEEN

'I should like permission to travel to Bitges, señor,' Alvarez said over the phone.

'Why?' demanded Salas.

'Before coming to the island, Señor Lewis stayed in Bitges. I know that because he ate in

133

a restaurant two days before catching a train from there to Barcelona.'

There was a short pause. 'It astonishes me the frequency with which you try to produce cause to travel around the world.'

'Bitges is in the province of Gerona . . .'

'Don't be insolent. Naturally, I know where it is.'

'I'm sorry, señor, but the way you put things did seem to suggest . . .'

'I suggested nothing . . . Why would there be the slightest relevance to Lewis's stay in Bitges?'

'It's such an odd place for him to be. It's fifty kilometres from the coast and very few foreigners go there, let alone stay there, so why did he when he was unable to speak any Castilian, let alone Catalan? The coast would have been a far more logical place for him to be. I can think of only one reason—he was brought over from England to do something illegal and he carefully based himself away from the scene of operations. Whatever that something was, he did it and was paid. A spendthrift, the money ran out and he set about finding more through blackmailing the person for whom he'd committed the criminal act—Clough. By visiting Bitges, I may be able to find out if I'm right. If I am, then there's a chance of uncovering evidence which will prove Clough was responsible for both Lewis's and Sheard's murders.'

'Put a request through to Bitges for inquiries to be made.'

'Señor, speed has to be of the essence if we are to discover the truth before it becomes too hidden ever to be revealed. If we ask Bitges to handle the inquiries, they'll merely shunt our request to one side since it is not a matter that directly concerns them . . .'

'You have no authority for making so damning an accusation.'

'When we receive a request from the Peninsula—'

'It is dealt with as a matter of priority.'

'Of course. But I have been told by many how unusual this is and how efficiently the department must be run.'

After a slight pause, Salas said: 'You will conduct as brief an inquiry as possible and on your return submit a detailed list of your expenses, verified by receipts.' He rang off.

Alvarez replaced the receiver. When a man heard words of honey, he seldom wondered why they'd been spoken.

*　　　*　　　*

Two brandies had been insufficient to anaesthetize him to the dangers of the half-hour flight and after arrival at Barcelona airport he felt the need of another at one of the bars before catching the shuttle to Sants station. There, he bought a ticket for the talgo

135

to Bitges.

On a clear day, the Pyrenees could be seen from Bitges and frequently in May, or even early June, their snow-clad peaks provided a sharp visual contrast to the hot, dusty town. Known for its textiles, it was also the home of numerous small businesses, many of which manufactured swords and knives. To the east of the town were the few stretches of Roman wall which previous generations had not dismantled to use the stone to build houses; to the north and half a kilometre outside, built around a natural hollow, were the remains of a Roman theatre. According to most Spaniards, the inhabitants were typical Catalans, dour rather than lively, suspicious of outsiders, and so sharp in money matters that they'd pursue a single peseta to hell; as seen by themselves, they were slow to make friends but the best of friends, honest, industrious businessmen, and far more generous in spirit than the selfish bastards of Madrid, Seville, Valladolid, or Bilbao.

Alvarez paid the taxi and crossed the pavement to enter the square building that had mullioned windows and heavily overhanging eaves which were peculiar to the area. He spoke to the duty receptionist, had to wait less than five minutes before being directed up to the third floor and Comisario Robles's office.

Robles was short, thin, nervously active and abrupt of speech. 'You're from Llueso? A lovely spot. I had a holiday there a few years ago with the family . . . Sit down. D'you smoke?'

'Regrettably, señor.'

'My father has smoked forty cigarettes a day since he was a youngster and never has as much as a cold.' He offered a pack, accepted a light, returned to his seat behind the desk on which were several neatly stacked files. 'So?'

Alvarez gave him a brief résumé of the facts and interpretations he placed on them.

'It's a tall order to hope you'll find out what's been going on when so much is guesswork.'

'I know, señor, but I'm banking on the belief that Lewis's base was here, though he spent considerable time elsewhere, probably the coast—that would mean he almost certainly hired a car. The garage may be able to give us some indication as to where he went and then the police records for that area can be checked to identify a crime in which he may well have been involved.'

'I trust you are an optimist.'

*   *   *

It proved to be a long weekend. Alvarez sat at many cafés, ate several meals in restaurants; he wandered through the large street market; he visited the museum which contained a wide selection of early textiles and textile machinery, ceremonial swords and daggers, and Roman artefacts; he even paid five hundred pesetas to see an exhibition of paintings by a local painter who had died in the forties and whose work was described in the catalogue as that of an unacknowledged genius—his considered opinion was that the lack of acknowledgment suggested the general public possessed more common sense than it was generally accorded.

On Monday morning he received a phone call from the comisario's secretary. Both the hotel at which Señor Lewis had stayed and the garage from which he'd hired a car had been identified and it was suggested that Inspector Alvarez meet Inspector Calvo at Garaje Fiol Roca in half an hour's time.

For once, he was glad to resume work. A short taxi ride took him to a modern building with large showrooms in the main shopping area. As he paid the taxi, a younger man, sleekly handsome but with an expression of humour to suggest he never took himself too seriously, came forward. 'Alvarez? . . . I'm Emiliano Calvo.' He shook hands energetically as the taxi drove off. 'I gather you're from Mallorca, which means Salas is the superior chief. Your bad luck is everyone else's good luck!'

Alvarez warmed to the other. 'You obviously know him.'

'Served under him before he moved to the island. I started each day by calling on the Almighty to arrange a little accident for him—

nothing serious, just sufficient to incapacitate him permanently. It never happened, of course. The more urgent the plea, the less it's listened to . . . Let's get out of the sun and I'll give you the facts.'

They moved into the shade of an overhead awning. Calvo brought a notebook out of his trouser pocket, opened it. 'Lewis booked in at the Hotel Gandia on the twenty-ninth of May; he came here on the thirtieth and hired a Renault 19. He left the hotel on the eighth of June and returned the car the same day . . . I suggested coming here first because it's nearer our place and there's a small cafe around the corner which serves the best coffee in town.'

They entered the building, walked between two gleaming saloons and a small sports car and into a glass-walled office in which a middle-aged man and a young woman worked at desks.

Calvo shook hands and introduced Alvarez.

'What's the problem this time?' asked the manager, harassed and hoping they would not bother him for long.

'I believe you hired a car to Señor Lewis in May,' Alvarez said. 'Can you remember him?'

'Only very vaguely. I'd only know him if he started speaking.'

'How's that?'

Neither he nor Teresa, his secretary, had been able to understand a word of what he'd been saying. In desperation, they'd called in one of the mechanics who'd always claimed to be fluent in English. That had turned out to be a gross exaggeration, but with his help they had finally managed to understand that the Englishman wanted to hire a car for nine days. They'd provided a blue Renault 19. At the end of a week he'd returned and—again with the aid of the mechanic—reported a slight fault which had easily been rectified.

'Did he talk about what he was doing?'

'You'd better ask Teresa. She'd more time to try and understand at least something of what he said,' the manager answered.

Alvarez turned. 'Did he, señorita?'

'I'm not sure what you mean.'

'Did he mention why he was staying in Bitges and why he wanted a car?'

'We never got round to talking about things like that.'

'Did he ever mention anywhere he'd been?'

'He didn't say anything he didn't have to; leastwise, if he did, I didn't understand it.'

'How many kilometres had the car covered when he returned it?'

She looked at the manager. He nodded. She tapped out instructions on the keyboard of the PC, studied the VDU. 'It was just over one thousand four hundred kilometres.'

Alvarez mentally considered the figures. The distance to the coast was roughly fifty kilometres, so had Lewis driven down there and back each day, he'd have covered nine hundred kilometres; that left five hundred for shorter journeys . . .

Alvarez thanked them for their help.

*   *   *

The Hotel Gandia was new, without any particular character, and run with cold efficiency. The assistant manager, possessing the belligerence of an undersized, slightly rat-faced man determined to assert his importance to the world, tried to object to the staff's being questioned and it was only after Calvo had applied a degree of pressure that he reluctantly agreed.

A waiter, middle-aged and pot-bellied, certainly remembered the Englishman because it had been so difficult to understand what he'd wanted on the few occasions he'd eaten in the restaurant. Still, he had proved to be more generous than some . . .

A chambermaid, in her late twenties, with a face sadly disfigured by a broad scar across her right cheek that lifted the corner of her mouth, was more helpful. 'If he saw me, he always had a chat.'

'Then you speak English, senorita?' Alvarez said.

'I've been learning because one day I want to travel and see some of the world and the only way I can do that is if I get work. English is so important . . .'

141

Alvarez was sure there was heartache behind her words. Without her facial disfigurement, she would have been pleasant-looking. She would have married and had a family, still the average Spanish woman's ambition. But because young men seldom bothered to look for inner beauty, she saw little hope of marriage. 'Did the senor ever tell you why he was staying in Bitges?'

'Never said anything about that.'

'This is important, so see if you can remember. Did he ever mention where he was going or where he'd been locally?'

Time passed. 'I don't think so.'

'Did he ask you where any place was?'

She shook her head.

He thought for a moment, then said: 'D'you think he went swimming?'

'He must have done. Quite often his costume would be hanging up to dry out on the balcony.'

'Is there a swimming pool in the town?'

Calvo answered. 'There's one at the sports centre.'

'So he might have gone swimming there or down at the coast.' Alvarez spoke to her once more. 'Let's suppose he went to the coast to swim. You can't think of anything to suggest where that might have been?'

She hesitated.

'You might be able to help us?'

'If Señor Pons hears about it . . .'

'The assistant manager will learn nothing from us.'

'He's so stupid about it. Saying he's to be told immediately so he can order the guest to leave. I mean, he knows that in any hotel men take women to their rooms. But the way he goes on . . . To be honest, I reckon he has a kinky interest in it.'

'You're saying that Señor Lewis had a lady in his room?'

'There was no notice on the door and it was well into the morning so I just went straight in. They were both in one of the beds . . . Must have been real tired after a busy night to be able to sleep that cramped,' she added, with a touch of earthy humour.

'Then you woke them?'

'Of course, since I wasn't trying to be quiet.'

'How did they react?'

'He wasn't the kind to be worried. She was very upset, but it seemed that was just because of the time. I'm only learning English and she was talking real fast, but I think she was telling him that if she wasn't at the Colón in half an hour to greet the new guests, she'd lose her job . . . You're sure you won't tell Señor Pons about it?'

'You have my word.'

'It's just that if he heard, he'd give me hell for not telling him about it. Might even sack me.' Her voice sharpened. 'If his uncle didn't own the hotel, he'd not crow so loud.'

'Perhaps his uncle will die and leave it to his mistress.'

'Life never works that fairly . . . Why are you asking all these questions about the señor?'

'Sadly, he was murdered in Mallorca. I have to try and discover who killed him.'

'Murdered? . . . And he was so alive.'

CHAPTER SIXTEEN

There were times when one had to be sufficiently optimistic to hope that another's sense of logic was the same as one's own. If, Alvarez decided, he were English, staying in Bitges, and looking for female company, he'd make for the nearest seaside resort. He opened a map and spread this out on the bed. The only main road in the area ran eastwards from Bitges to Playa de Samallera, which made the latter the nearest resort both by distance and time. Playa de Samallera lay on a bay that was ringed by mountains and so the next resort on either side—which would be reached by driving through Playa de Samallera unless one enjoyed mountaineering—was more distant both in kilometres and time. So while it might he possible to drive to Playa in half an hour, it was certainly impossible to reach anywhere else along the coast.

The local police in Playa de Samallera were less than helpful. 'In the height of summer when there are more tourists than fleas on a dog and most of 'em causing twice as much trouble?'

'It shouldn't be difficult,' Alvarez said peacefully. 'There's surely not more than one Hotel Colón and there can't be many English-speaking reps who work there.'

'How would you know whether it's going to be difficult or impossible? You come from a sleepy island where a drunken tourist is a novelty.'

'We suffer twice as many tourists in a year as the whole of the Costa Brava.'

They called him a liar.

*   *   *

Designed by an architect who had been an admirer of Gaudí, but blessed with the ability of knowing when to stop, Hotel Colón was a place of odd angles, unusual slopes, and peculiar surfaces, which attracted attention but not necessarily incomprehension. It catered for upmarket holidaymakers and the foyer was a place of space, curving arches, and a fountain in which swam a number of very large goldfish. The staff wore a uniform of light fawn linen jacket, white shirt, blue tie or neck scarf, and dark fawn linen trousers or skirt.

The receptionist said: 'The local police have been on to us and we've had a word with the female tour representatives who work here. Señorita Dunn is a friend of Señor Lewis.'

Alvarez knew the warm pleasure of attaining success against the odds. 'Is she in the hotel at the moment?'

'I've no idea, but she's usually around during the afternoon so I'll have her paged.'

'Thanks. Where can I have a word with her?'

'At this time of the afternoon, the lounge is usually empty.'

Through the picture window of the lounge, Alvarez saw a curving stretch of sand, sea, and the southern half of the bay backed by mountains with roller-coaster peaks. Despite the crowds, the multicoloured beach umbrellas, the Tahiti sun cones, and the armada of power and pedal boats, it was a scene of beauty. Though not, of course, anywhere near as beautiful as Llueso Bay.

He sat in one of the comfortable armchairs and relaxed . . .

'Are you the policeman who wants to speak to me?'

Jerked fully awake, he looked up. She was sufficiently young and attractive to make him regret that he could look back on so many years. Her hair was blonde, eyes blue, mouth generous; she wore just above her right breast a name tab. A man could spend a long time reading her name . . . Rather late in the day, he remembered the English custom and stood. 'Señorita Dunn?'

'Yes,' she answered in Spanish.

'My name is Inspector Enrique Alvarez, from Mallorca.'

'Why are you . . .' She came to a stop, unable to find immediately the word she wanted.

'I speak English, señorita. Would that be easier?'

She smiled briefly. 'It would, only don't tell my boss. As far as he's concerned, like all reps, I'm totally fluent in Spanish and even not bad in Catalan.' Her tone changed. 'The local police asked me if I knew Neil Lewis. If you're here because of him, why? What's going on?'

'Shall we sit and I will explain.'

A waiter looked through the doorway, came across to ask if they wanted something to drink.

'I wouldn't mind a coffee,' she said.

'Two coffees,' Alvarez ordered. Then he added: 'And a coñac.'

As the waiter left, she said; 'Well, what is this all about?'

'Señorita, I much regret I have to tell you that Señor Lewis is dead.'

'My God!'

He saw surprise, but not shocked grief. He was grateful for this. The hardest part of his job was to have to give news that so obviously introduced tragedy into someone's life.

'I suppose he had a car accident? I always

said he would.'

'It was no accident. He was on a boat when he was murdered.'

'Christ!' She began to fidget with the arms of the chair. 'Who? Why?'

'It is to try to find the answers that I am here.'

Her voice rose. 'You can't think I killed him?'

'Of course not, señorita.'

'Then how ... Look, how did you ever discover I knew him?'

'I learned in Bitges that he was friendly with someone who was probably working for an English travel company. That suggested you worked here, in Playa de Samallera.'

'I suppose it was the chambermaid at the Gandia who told you. She kept apologizing the day she burst into the room and we were both asleep in bed, but I was sure that inside she was laughing ...' She stared into the distance.

The waiter returned, placed coffee, milk jug, sugar bowl, and a glass of brandy, on the table, left. She did not move. Alvarez helped himself to milk and sugar, drank enough coffee to be able to pour the brandy into the cup.

She said suddenly: 'I'm sorry, I was miles away.' She helped herself to milk, but not sugar. 'How was he killed?'

'He was dragged off the boat and held underwater.'

'God, someone didn't like him!'

148

'I think that is because he was trying to blackmail his murderer.' He watched her. 'You don't seem very surprised at the possibility?'

'I'm not—That's one hell of a bitchy thing to say, isn't it?'

'If it's the truth, it is not bitchy.'

'Is that necessarily so? Never mind, I'll believe it is in order to keep my conscience happy.'

'Why does it not surprise you that Señor Lewis may have been blackmailing someone?'

'Because there was something about Neil that made me think . . . well, that he didn't operate to the normal limits. Does that sound daft? The thing is, in my job one gets to have a feeling about people very quickly. When I meet an incoming flight, it's no time before I mentally sort everyone out into easy and pleasant, bloody-minded and complaining, and wandering hands. I'm seldom wrong, especially over the last category.'

'And you judged Lewis to be a criminal?'

'No. At least, not in those sort of terms. I thought he was always ready to act recklessly, so if he wanted something, he'd go hell-bent after it and forget the consequences. To be real corny, there was a touch of the buccaneer about him.'

'Have you any idea why he was staying in Bitges?'

'No, none.'

'Perhaps he knew someone who lives in the

area?'

'If he did, he never mentioned them.'

'Do you know where he went when he left here?'

'He said Barcelona and that he'd get in touch. He didn't, of course.' She showed no resentment. She drained her cup. 'Is that all? I'm sorry to rush, but very soon I have to be on show so that the punters can ask me stupid questions.'

He smiled.

'You don't believe they do? Yesterday, a woman came up and complained bitterly that the noticeboard said Patricia Dunn would be on duty every afternoon to answer customers' questions, but she was never around. I showed her my name tag—resisting the urge to ask if she could read—and politely asked how I could help. "I only wanted to make certain you're where they said you'd be."' She stood. 'I wish I could have helped you find whoever killed Neil. He was fun.'

As she walked to the doorway, he thought it was odd how often women were attracted by the hint, but not the reality, of lawlessness.

When he had finished the coffee and brandy, the waiter entered and presented the bill. One thousand and fifty pesetas. Small wonder, he thought sourly as he paid and asked for a receipt, that the hotel possessed an air of luxury.

On his way across the foyer, he saw Patricia,

standing by a noticeboard, and was inexplicably seized with the childish urge to go across and ask her a stupid question. 'Why do the locals speak a funny language?'

'So that you won't be upset by learning what they think of you.'

He smiled. 'Goodbye again, senorita. It has been a pleasure knowing you.'

'And meeting you.'

He began to walk away.

'Hey, hang on a sec!' she called out.

He returned to her side.

'Your complaining about the locals not speaking English suddenly reminded me of something. I don't know if it's of any account, but soon after I met Neil, he turned up one evening in a hell of a temper and said he'd been trying to find an address but everyone he asked for directions was an idiot. It turned out he'd been so mispronouncing the name it was small wonder no one could understand that he was looking for Pellapuig.'

'Is that a village?'

'An urbanización along the coast.'

'Did he say why he'd been trying to find the place or name anyone who lived there?'

She shook her head.

*　　　*　　　*

Once again, the local police were less than immediately helpful. 'You expect us to identify someone who lives in Pellapuig when you don't know the name or address?'

'The person is probably English.'

'That'll be a great help when the English are the only bastards rich enough and stupid enough to live in such a place!'

'You have the photograph I've given you to show people. It's worth a try.'

'Yeah? Only because it's not you what's got to do the trying.'

CHAPTER SEVENTEEN

The house was large and Catalan in style, with two round towers. Its setting was dramatic. The land ended in a sheer, hundred-metre cliff and the south face of the house was within ten metres of the edge.

Alvarez knocked on the front door. It was opened by a woman in her forties who looked to be in her sixties because her skin had been tanned and wrinkled by summer sun and winter wind. He introduced himself, said he'd like a chat with her. She made it obvious she would not welcome a chat with him. 'There's no reason to be concerned,' he assured her.

'I told the policeman when he came here that I didn't know who the man was. He called me a liar and said I was trying to pervert justice, whatever that means.'

'He didn't know what he was talking about.' He smiled.

She was reassured by his easy, friendly manner. 'I suppose you'd best come in.'

He entered a hall that was barely furnished. 'Is it right that this house is owned by someone in Barcelona who lets it to tourists during the summer? Must make the odd peseta doing that.'

'If I had what he gets in the season, I wouldn't be doing this job!'

As he had immediately judged, she was from a peasant background. This enabled him further to gain her confidence by introducing subjects that would most interest her. They briefly discussed the inequalities of life, the inequalities of the lottery—it was always the wrong people who won it—and the poor prices farmers received.

She asked him if he'd like some coffee, led the way into a kitchen that was only basically equipped. She filled a sauce-pan with water and put this on the gas stove, then said she always brought a merienda to work but seldom finished it and would he like some? They shared a large spinach empanada and when he praised it as one of the best he had ever eaten, the last of her reserve vanished. Her husband had always liked her empanadas. She talked about the rented farm she and her husband had worked and how, when her husband had suddenly died, the tenancy had come to an end.

She'd had to earn a living, so she'd found a job with the company that let houses to tourists. It was boring work, lacking any sense of satisfaction—not like growing things—but it provided the money necessary to see her two children through university. And sometimes the tourists were generous and gave her extra money which bought a luxury, or two . . .

'You remember the man whose photograph you were shown by the local police?'

She nodded.

'Who was renting this place when he called?'

'Two sisters. Leastwise, one of 'em was here all the time, the other only for a bit.'

'Tell me about them. What were their names?'

'Couldn't say.'

'You're not given a list of the people who'll be staying here?'

'The company just tells me when someone's coming.'

Her suddenly blanked expression suggested she could read only with the greatest difficulty—when she had been young, schooling had cost money and her family had probably not been able to afford even the few pesetas necessary. He would have liked to tell her that far from feeling shame because she could not read, she should be proud that she had done everything possible to make certain her children had a full education, but knew it would be kinder not to pursue the matter. 'So there was just the one sister to start with? What kind of person was she?'

She shrugged her shoulders.

'Pleasant?'

'Not really. Not like the other. Maybe they looked alike, except for the hair, but she acted like she was some great person's wife while the other was always friendly.'

'When did the second sister arrive here?'

'A few days later, just after the friend left.'

'What friend?'

'The man that stayed for three days.'

'Here, in the house?'

'Haven't I just said?'

'Where did he sleep?'

'Where d'you think?'

'With her?'

'Only he didn't want me to know, so he tried to make out he spent the night in the second bedroom.'

'How do you know he didn't?'

'I make the beds in the morning, don't I? His sheets were hardly ruffled, hers looked like the two of 'em had been running races.'

'Maybe he was a sound sleeper and she was a very restless one?'

'You think I can't tell after all the beds I've made for foreigners? In any case, once he'd left, her bed was different.'

'You've seen a photograph of Señor Lewis. Can you remember who was living here when he called that day?'

'The two of 'em.'

'Which two?' he asked patiently.

'The sisters.'

'Tell me about his visit.'

She had a peasant's memory for details. She'd been sweeping down the patio, because there'd been a wind which had brought sand from Africa, when there'd been a ring on the front door bell. The señoras had been out. The Englishman had been so stupid he couldn't understand what she'd been trying to tell him even though she'd spoken as simply as if to a child. In the end, without a word of thanks or even a smile, he'd driven off.

'Did he return another time?'

She shrugged her shoulders. 'Didn't see him again.'

'How did the two sisters get on together?'

The question puzzled her, so he simplified it.

'They seemed to be friendly enough,' she said.

'Did they leave together?'

'Must have done.'

'Why do you say that?'

'The let ended on my rest day, so they was gone when I returned to get the house ready for the next lot.'

He finished his coffee, put the mug down on the kitchen table. 'Can you describe the sisters and the male friend?'

She found it more difficult than most to provide word pictures. They weren't young any

156

more, but didn't look old—when you hadn't worked in the fields, you could hide the years much more easily. The blonde had used lots of make-up, the black-haired sister hardly any; one dressed up, the other hadn't seemed to mind what clothes she wore. The one was as mean as a lawyer from Santiago—she'd not left as much as a peseta in her bedroom; the other was the most generous of señoras and left twenty thousand—yes, twenty thousand. No other señora had ever approached such generosity. The money had bought her son a new jacket which he'd been needing for a long time . . .

As he listened to her, he gloomily realized that if he possessed any intelligence, before he'd left the island he would have obtained a photograph of Vera Clough. 'Tell me about the señor.'

He was something of a hidalgo. Pleasant, but kind of distant; smartly dressed; often smiling, but usually with his mouth and not his eyes.

'Did he have a neat moustache?'

She looked at him with some surprise. 'How did you know that?'

*　　　*　　　*

He drove back to Playa de Samallera and eventually found a parking space, but much further from the letting agency's offices than he would have wished. The walk left him sweating

157

profusely.

'Are you all right?' said the young woman behind the counter.

He mopped his face with a handkerchief. 'I hope so,' he answered breathlessly. 'Cuerpo General de Policia. Will you give me the names of the tourists who hired Casa Escarpa in the Pellapuig urbanización in May and June.'

'Sure ... Why don't you sit down while I look through the files.'

He sat, still breathing heavily. He wondered if all his promises to diet, stop smoking, and drink less, were about to levy their price for his having repeatedly broken them; was his heart about to tear itself apart ...?

'Here we are,' she said, as she studied the VDU. 'Shall I print them out for you?'

All the bookings had been made in the UK and with one exception in the names of couples; that exception was for a booking from 25 May to 8 June, by Mrs F. Dewar.

CHAPTER EIGHTEEN

Television had introduced the outside world to the inhabitants of Llueso, but not necessarily eradicated the belief that it was an alien, dangerous place. Dolores hugged Alvarez as if he were indeed lucky to have returned home. When she finally released him, she said; 'Jaime

158

took me to the fishmonger in Playa Neuva early this morning so I could make you Oblades amb bolets for lunch. You like that, don't you?'

'Cooked by you, it is a slice of heaven.' That was true. No one could prepare turbot as she could.

'And I've bought two bottles of Gran Coronas to enjoy with it.'

Had any man ever enjoyed so rich a homecoming?

*   *   *

In the conventional sense, Son Preda was not a beautiful house, but for him, especially seen in the early evening sunshine, it possessed an attraction no palace could because it had so obviously been built to serve the land, not impress people.

The elder maid opened the front door and showed him into the room with the flintlock rifles on the walls. Within the minute, Clough entered. 'Good evening.'

'I am sorry to trouble you again, señor, but I have one or two more questions to ask.'

'Without questions, a detective would be like a car with no petrol ... I'm glad you've called because I want to say that when I spoke to you over the phone the other day I'm sure I sounded very discourteous. The fact is, my wife was upset by your visit and that made me unsettled; always does. I'm sure you'll understand.'

'But of course, señor.'

'Good. Then before we come to the "one or two questions", let me get you a drink. What would you like?'

'A coñac with just ice, if I may.'

'Grab a seat while I go and get it.'

Once seated, Alvarez let his mind wander. The gods had showered their gifts; he was the owner of Son Preda. He would call back the older men who had lost faith in themselves because they had been made redundant either by rising costs or mechanization and he would restore that faith by employing them on the estate. They would harvest the almonds, algarrobos, and olives with long bamboos, their wrists and forearms once more picking up the rhythm of the work . . .

The door opened and a woman entered the room in a rush, came to a sudden halt. 'I thought Larry was here.'

He always had difficulty in judging a woman's age, but was reasonably certain she was in her middle twenties. Reasonably attractive, was his immediate assessment, but only in a very un-Spanish manner—she lacked any sense of groomed, smooth sophistication. Her bouncy golden hair, deep blue eyes, freckled face, pert nose, and generous mouth provided the gamin appearance that seemed so popular in more northerly and less critical climes. He said: 'Señor Clough left a moment ago. I am sure he will be returning very soon.'

'Then I'll wait. By the way, I'm Phoebe Owen.'

'My name is Enrique Alvarez, señorita.'

'Isn't Enrique the Spanish for Henry?'

'I believe so.'

Clough entered, two glasses on a silver salver. 'Hullo, Phoebe. Not roasting yourself?'

'I decided I'd better come out of the sun for a while.'

'Signs of common sense?'

'Signs, but no certainty.'

He smiled. 'I see you've met the inspector.'

'He didn't say he was an inspector. Of police?'

Clough put one glass down on the occasional table by Alvarez's side. 'Of the Cuerpo General de Policia, if I remember correctly ... I'm sorry, but I'm going to have to suggest you wander, Phe. The inspector's here on business.'

'He's going to arrest you?'

'I hope not; not with the golf tournament fast approaching and a thousand peseta bet on myself ... If you see Vera, tell her that if she'd like a drink, I've put three or four bottles of champagne in the fridge.'

'Will do.' She left.

Clough sat. 'She's a distant cousin, but I can never remember how many times removed. Over here for sun and solace. When one yearns to be young again, one forgets that that would mean suffering endless emotional upsets once

161

more . . . Now, how can I help you?'

'Do you know Señora Fenella Dewar?'

He drank, held the glass in his hand and stared down at it for several seconds, then looked up at Alvarez. 'My sister-in-law. Now tell me, why should you be the slightest bit interested in whether or not we know each other?'

'I have been making inquiries and learned that the señora rented Casa Escarpa in the Pellapuig urbanizacíon which is near Playa de Samallera, south of Barcelona.'

'I see.'

'I understand your wife stayed with Señora Dewar at Casa Escarpa.'

'Indeed. And had a pleasant few days, despite their being sisters.'

'They are not as companionable as one might hope?'

'Sibling rivalries are far more common than idealists would have us believe. Unfortunately, my sister-in-law is of a very jealous nature.'

'Did you visit Casa Escarpa?'

'Yes.'

'At a time when your wife was not there?'

'That's right.'

'Does your wife know about your visit?'

Clough smiled. 'Professional experience forces you to suspect the worst? In this case, without justification. Business problems had been dragging on and I decided on a direct approach to the people concerned and flew out

162

to Würzburg. It was a hard slog, hut I got most of what I wanted. I went from Frankfurt to Barcelona and hired a car to drive down to Pellapuig, expecting to find my wife at the house. Instead, I learned she'd cancelled her flight from England. Naturally worried, I phoned to find out what was wrong and she told me she'd suffered a nasty bout of migraine and simply wasn't up to travelling yet. I told her I'd get back as soon as I could find a flight, but she insisted I stay for a few days because she reckoned I needed the break, even if short. In the event, I had to leave before she arrived.'

'I spoke to Susana and she . . .'

'Who's Susana?'

'The maid who worked in the house.'

'D'you know, this is the first time I've learned her name! I tried to communicate with her, but with conspicuous and often amusing lack of success.'

'She suggested to me that Señora Dewar and you shared the same bed.'

Clough laughed.

'It is not true?'

'I'd have to think very hard to suggest something less likely.'

'She told me that each morning your bed was so little disturbed you could not have slept in it all night, whereas the señora's bed was in a state of considerable disturbance.'

'I am a peaceful sleeper; obviously, Fenella is a very restless one.'

'I suggested this to Susana. She said that the señora's bed was very much less disturbed after you'd left.'

'She sounds to me like a frustrated woman eager to read all sorts of things into a creased sheet. Is she married?'

'She is a widow.'

'There's the explanation. But maybe it'll be best if you have a word with my wife; she can confirm the impossibility of my having an affair with Fenella.'

'For the moment, there is no need to disturb her.'

'She'll be amused, not disturbed. In any case, sooner or later you're going to demand to talk to her, so why not now?'

'Why do you say that?'

'You'll want to know why she's been lying as well as I.'

Alvarez hoped he didn't look as surprised as he felt. The next question showed he had.

'You went to Pellapuig because you learned that Neil had been there. Isn't that so?'

'In a way.'

'Surely, in every way? ... I'll find Vera.' He left.

Alvarez drained his glass. His ace had been well and truly trumped.

Clough returned with Vera. She greeted Alvarez briefly, sat on one of the armchairs, said; 'Larry, can I have a drink?'

'I told Phe to offer you champagne, but

164

obviously she didn't find you. I'll do the honours and at the same time recharge our glasses.' He picked up Alvarez's glass and his own, left the room again.

She nervously faced Alvarez. 'Larry says you seem to believe it possible that my sister and he were having an affair?'

'Señora, perhaps you would prefer to wait until your husband returns before we discuss the matter?'

'No, I would not.'

He was surprised by the sudden firmness with which she spoke.

'You have to understand how ridiculous the suggestion is and I'll find it a little easier to explain if he's not here. When we were young, my sister was always belle of the ball. Do you understand that?'

'I think so.'

'Because of her looks and vivacity, the handsome men always made a beeline for her at parties. She married Tancred and her life was what she'd always demanded, big house, big parties, endless trips abroad. But after a few years, he disappeared with another woman and it turned out that his wealth was largely illusory. My sister wasn't left penniless, but compared to how things had been, she was not well off. A little later, my husband, whom she'd always considered very dull, died and left me a fortune. I'm afraid that that made her very jealous. So when I married Larry, who was so

165

successful, her feelings reached the stage where she said things that were really unforgivable. But she is my sister so I tried to stay friendly and for my sake Larry never told her what he thought of her behaviour; thankfully, over the last couple of years she's almost learned to come to terms with the way things are and we've grown closer together. But although Larry has been wonderful in hiding his true feelings, he's never forgotten or forgiven. So you see, she really is the very last person in the world with whom he'd have an affair.'

'Thank you for telling me, señora.'

Clough returned. He filled a flute with champagne, handed this to his wife, then a glass to Alvarez. He sat.

'I've explained how things are with Fenella,' she said.

Clough faced Alvarez. 'Then you're satisfied I stayed firmly in my own bed and the maid has rather too energetic an imagination?'

'Yes, señor.'

'So you're left with the question, why did we lie about Neil? . . . Will everything we say now be in confidence?'

'Unless that should become necessary, it will not be repeated.'

'Fair enough . . . Before Tancred married Fenella, he'd fathered a child. The mother was from a wealthy county family who were sufficiently reactionary not to be in favour of one-parent families and as soon as the baby was born, he was adopted. As you'll have guessed, the adopting parents' name was Lewis.

'We don't know anything about life at home, but obviously something, somewhere was wrong. Neil started mixing with the wrong crowd and ended up in trouble. He claimed his conviction so shocked him . . .'

Vera cut in. 'Why are you so grudging?'

'Because I look at things far more realistically than you do, my sweet. Still, whichever way you look at them, he decided to trace his true parents—a task that now is, I believe, easier than it used to be. He managed to identify both his father and mother. She flatly denied he was her child and refused to have anything to do with him. No one knew where his father was, but through the marriage he traced Fenella. By lucky chance—from his point of view—he arrived at her house on a day when my wife was there. Neil—arrogant and blaming everyone but himself for his problems—immediately put Fenella's back up, but my wife . . .'

She interrupted him a second time. 'He was gritty, but it was obvious that he'd had a rough life and one had to feel sorry for him.'

'You'd summon up sympathy for Jack the Ripper.'

'That's stupid . . . I felt certain that a little help might save him, so I offered him some money.'

'Having been warned by Fenella not to.'

'It can't be wrong to try and help someone.'

'Sadly, a recipe for disaster.' He spoke to Alvarez once more. 'Events were predictable. In May, he turned up again with a further hard-luck story and a plea for more money. My wife had recovered and was just about to fly out to Barcelona, so she told him to get in touch when she returned and she'd talk to me and see what best to do.

'Neil could be certain what my advice would be so he decided to try and circumvent my objections. He turned up in Pellapuig, unfortunately after I'd left, pleading that if he wasn't helped financially, he'd be forced to return to crime. Fenella told him that that was his problem; my wife gave him more money. Naturally, Fenella went on and on telling my wife how silly she'd been; probably becoming so heated because she reckoned she should have had first grab and had her holiday for free.'

'Which just shows how wrong you are when you're so quick to think the worst of people,' Vera said. 'Her holiday didn't cost her anything.'

'Because you paid for it?'

'Yes.'

'I should have guessed. Your generosity is only exceeded by your vulnerability.'

'You know how I hate it when you say things like that.'

'When I see you being taken for a ride

168

because of your good nature . . . Enough of the family bickering, which is almost as boring for third parties as family jokes . . . The next time Neil surfaced was when he arrived here one morning. Lacking imagination, his story hadn't changed—bad luck had robbed him, he was once more penniless and desperately trying to escape the clutches of crime, give him some money and he'd find a job and become a decent citizen.'

'Why did you believe him this time?'

'I haven't said I did.'

'Surely the story about giving your wife's dressmaker the million pesetas was a lie?'

'Of course. But I'd never expected to be challenged on that point and had to think up an explanation on the spot. No, I didn't believe him any more than I had previously.'

'Then why give him the money?'

For the first time, Clough showed some hesitation. 'The gods call on us to know ourselves. It's easy for them since, being gods, whatever they find in themselves must be virtuous. It's different for us mortals. Knowing ourselves can make us . . . A rambling way of trying to avoid the humiliating admission that I place far more value on social standing than is reasonable. In mitigation, I can only plead that when I was young, there was never enough money in the house. Poverty—even when relative—leaves a lasting mark. But since most things are double-sided, it can also breed a fierce determination to succeed. It's boasting, but I've succeeded in life.

'Arriving on this island, it didn't take long to understand that although the expatriate community doesn't have many social levels, it is very far from a classless society. I gather that some years ago, the traditional birth and breeding were the entrée into the top rank, but, as in most other places, standards have declined and money has become the prime requisite. Live in a large house, drive an expensive car, preferably of German manufacture, and one is virtually received anywhere, however boorish one's character. We were received without question—though I hope not despite a tendency to boorishness.

'When a society measures social values by perceived wealth, its members are never at ease because money, unlike breeding, has no inbuilt permanency; in the old days, the aristocrat could shrug off any number of scandals; the modern parvenu—unless in the entertainment world—dreads even the whiff of one. I was convinced that if people learned that our nephew—which, of course, Neil was not, but gossip prefers fiction to fact—was a convicted criminal, they would tend to ostracize us, at the same time rejoicing in the fact that they did not have criminal nephews. To avoid this, I gave Neil the money on condition he moved out of our lives.'

'But you have said that each time he made a

170

promise, you disbelieved him.'

'Because my judgement was not clouded by personal considerations. When it was, I denied all logic and somehow found it possible to hope.'

'Did you see Señor Lewis again after you gave him the money?'

'No. I hoped he'd left the island right up to the time you told us he was missing.'

'That was, perhaps, not unwelcome news?'

Clough smiled bitterly. 'A barbed question! Do I accept your assessment and incur your even sharper regard, or deny it and risk being branded a hypocrite?'

Alvarez was silent for a moment, then said: 'Thank you for being so frank.' He stood.

'I hope you can now appreciate why we both lied to you?'

Vera said: 'The fact is, Inspector, you never did believe me, did you?'

'Señora, I never disbelieve a lady until I am forced to do so.'

'Gallant, but hardly an answer.'

Alvarez said goodbye to Vera and followed Clough through the hall and outside. As he crossed to his car, Phoebe appeared around the side of the house. 'Are you arresting Larry?' she asked gaily.

'No, señorita.'

'What a pity!'

Clough said wryly: 'Do you have to be quite so disappointed?'

'But it would have given me something to write to Wendy about.'

'Arrange your own arrest to ensure a more vivid prose.'

'Why should the inspector arrest me?'

'Use your imagination.'

'And?'

'Why not try importuning?'

She faced Alvarez. 'Would you arrest me for that?'

'I am sorry, I do not know what it means.'

She laughed.

Feeling stupid, he climbed into the car and drove off.

CHAPTER NINETEEN

'Enrique,' Dolores said, 'you are looking sad.'

Alvarez ate the last spoonful of sopa torrada, checked the earthenware bowl and saw it had been emptied of the chicken and bread soup. If anything, he looked a little sadder.

'Is something the matter?' Her family was her life and the slightest hint of trouble to any member caused her concern.

'On Monday, I am going to have to phone the superior chief.'

'Monday's three days away,' Jaime said. 'Forget it until then.'

'How can I forget that in three days' time he is going to go on and on about how incompetent I am?'

'If he talks like that,' Dolores snapped, 'he has the wits of a cockroach. Why is such a man your superior chief?'

'Because the director-general appointed him.'

'Then the director-general is a bigger fool.'

'That's possible; they say he's more politician than policeman.'

'Why should the superior chief say you're incompetent?'

'I've recently cost the department a lot of wasted money.'

'They're government. What does the government ever do but waste money?'

'It wouldn't matter so much if it weren't now clear that the whole investigation has been a waste of time as well.'

'And is that your fault?'

'Not really.'

'Then you do not need to concern yourself.'

'The superior chief will make certain I am concerned.' Alvarez drained his glass. 'Anyway, perhaps the truth is that I am incompetent.'

'Stop speaking such nonsense!'

'A man with all his wits does not count the flock until certain all the sheep are his.'

'A man can only do what he thinks is right.' She stood, collected up the dirty plates and carried them through to the kitchen.

'I don't understand,' said Jaime, as he refilled his glass. He pushed the bottle of wine across the table. 'Who's lost the sheep?'

'What sheep?' Alvarez asked, his mind not on the question.

'The ones that have been stolen and you can't find.'

'I was just using sheep as a figure of speech. What I meant was, I should have made certain of all the facts before I propounded a theory to explain them.'

'I still don't understand.'

'I'm not certain I do either. There's no discernible motive for Lewis's murder, so what probably happened was that he went to the stern of the boat for a pee, fell overboard, and was too tight to save himself. Yet if that was the case, why was he drugged?'

'If he was stoned hollow, where's the problem?'

'Not that kind of drug. A Mickey Finn.'

'Never heard of it.'

'It's used to dope a potential victim's drink to make it easy to rob him. Lewis was definitely drugged, which virtually confirms that the others were as well.'

'What others?'

'His friend and two women.'

Jaime drank deeply and thought. 'You call yourself a detective?' he finally said, with heavy sarcasm. 'He meant to make it easy for him and his mate to have fun with the girls, but forgot what he'd put the dope into and drank it along with them. Never thought of that, I suppose?'

'Can't say I have. But if that's the way things were, how come there was no trace of dope in the remaining whisky and glasses?'

'How would I know? You think I'm going to do all your work for you?'

*   *   *

Always put off until tomorrow what does not have to be done today. Yet sometimes it had to be done. On Monday morning, Alvarez accepted he would have to ring the superior chief and therefore it would be only sensible to seek the comfort of a couple of brandies with his coffee at the Club Llueso before he did so. Sadly, they did not comfort him sufficiently to make his task any more welcome.

'The superior chief,' said the superior secretary, 'is not at work today.' Her tone became solemn. 'He is ill in bed.'

'Seriously ill?'

'You will be grateful to learn that although there is very considerable discomfort, there is no great danger. He strained his back playing golf.'

'Very unfortunate.'

'Indeed . . . Do you wish to speak to Comisario Borne who is temporarily in command?'

'I don't think so, thank you.'

He said goodbye and rang off. He opened the bottom righthand drawer of the desk and brought out the bottle and a glass. He poured himself his third brandy of the morning and drank to the game of golf.

*   *   *

He was walking along the lower part of the old square when a voice behind him said: 'Hullo again.' He turned to face Phoebe. 'Good afternoon, señorita.'

'Good evening, señor,' she replied, her tone mocking. 'Tell me, are you always so formal, or only to someone of whom you disapprove?'

'Why should I disapprove of you?'

'Because of my dreadful sense of humour. Although, in my defence, it was really Larry who was to blame. I told him we'd embarrassed you with the stupid joke, but he said you'd just laugh when you found out what "importuning" meant. Now you can tell me, who was right?'

'I was embarrassed by my ignorance, amused by your joke.'

'A tactful let-out, if ever I've heard one!' She smiled, then changed the subject. 'Larry brought me here yesterday morning and I thought the village so attractive I wanted to explore and then sit outside a café and linger over a drink, but he was in too much of a hurry, so I've come back to do just that today . . . I suppose you're on your way home?'

176

'Regretfully, no. I don't finish work until seven-thirty or eight.'

'I always forget that working hours here are so very different.'

It was interesting, he thought, how her straightforward, casually friendly manner so immediately identified her as either British or American. Had she been Spanish, or for that matter of any other continental nationality, in her bearing there would have been a hint of sexual query, if not provocation . . .

'Well, I mustn't keep you from your work any longer.'

There were aspects of the case which still perplexed him. Were he to offer her a drink, it would be natural to talk about matters of which they both had cognizance and, if he were careful, there should be no reason for her to suspect the true motive for his invitation. 'Señorita, I do not, for once, need to hurry back to my work, so perhaps I might offer you a drink to linger over?'

'That would be great. But on one condition: you remember I'm Phoebe, not "señorita".'

They climbed the steps to the levelled part of the square, crossed to where tables were set out, and sat under the shade of a tree. A waiter took their order.

She settled back in the chair. 'I wonder why it seems so natural to do this here, yet it becomes an affectation in England?'

'Perhaps because in Spain it is natural to do

what one enjoys doing.'

'Are you suggesting that back home it isn't?'

'I've always understood that the British feel it is sinful to enjoy too much pleasure.'

'That was long ago. Nowadays, commentators often say that the decline of the nation is due to our pursuing pleasure too hard.'

'Which surely shows an underlying disapproval?'

She laughed.

He noticed how the flesh about her eyes crinkled to extend the laugh right up her face. 'Are you staying on the island long?'

'Probably until Vera and Larry get fed up with me. At home . . . Let's just say, something happened and I needed to get away from everything. It's odd, but I feel more at rest when I'm with them than I do with my own family. I suppose it's because my family is usually squabbling, whereas they seem to agree about everything.'

This gave him the lead-in he'd wanted. 'I had the impression that they at least disagree about Señor Lewis.'

'Hardly surprising.'

'Why d'you say that?'

'Because when I met him, I took an immediate dislike to him. Cocky and aggressive.'

'Yet I understand Señora Clough was very kind to him?'

'From the day she first met him at Fenella's, she's let him take her for a ride, and that despite all Larry's warnings.'

'I suppose she was upset by his death?'

'Of course. She's no fool and I'm sure that in part she recognized him for what he was, but she's an incurable optimist and managed to hide that recognition by believing he could become what she wished him to be.' She paused, then said uncertainly: 'Am I beginning to sound like a wannabe psychologist?'

'Far from it. I think you understand people.'

'Sometimes. But never myself.' She stared into the distance.

His first summation had been wrong, he decided. True, by classical standards she was no great beauty, but her open looks possessed their own considerable charm . . . About to ask her a further question concerning the Cloughs and Lewis, he decided against doing so for fear she should suspect his stratagem. 'Would you like another drink?'

'D'you know, I'm afraid I really would! It's such fun just watching the world drift by.'

Lucky the man who brought her joy.

CHAPTER TWENTY

'What did the superior chief say?' Jaime asked, as he poured himself another drink.

Alvarez, who'd been deep in thought, looked up. 'What's that?'

Jaime repeated the question.

'I told you yesterday at lunch.'

'No, you didn't because I wasn't here.'

'Weren't you?'

'Seems you aren't all here now . . . Did the superior chief chew you up?'

'I didn't get to talk to him because he's off duty after doing in his back on a round of golf. Great game.'

Jaime drank deeply. 'About the problem of the whisky and the glasses. I've been thinking. You know what?'

'Tell me.'

'The bloke stayed awake longer than the women and cleaned everything up before he passed out so as they'd never know what he'd been up to. How's that?'

'Ingenious.'

The telephone rang. After a while, Dolores put her head through the bead curtain, stared at them, sighed, came through and hurried into the front room.

Jaime drained his glass. As he refilled it, he said: 'I've always reckoned I'd be good at your job. I mean, I notice things and I have ideas. That's all there is to it.'

'I suppose that's about right.'

There was the sound of shouting and Isabel, closely pursued by Juan, ran into the room. She swerved to avoid Alvarez's chair, cannoned

180

into the corner of the table and fell, began to whimper. Juan jeered at her. Forgetting her woes, she lashed out with her feet and caught him a blow on his left ankle that made him bellow with pain. As he hopped around, he called her several names, none of which was flattering.

'How dare you speak like that!' Dolores said from the doorway of the front room.

It was many days since her voice had held a note of such sharp authority. Juan hastened to excuse himself. 'I was . . .'

'Speaking filth.'

'She kicked me and nearly broke my ankle.'

'I didn't,' Isabel protested.

'Yes, you did.'

'You pushed me into the chair.'

'You ran into it because you're stupid.'

'Be quiet!' Dolores snapped. 'Juan, go to your room.'

'But . . .'

'One more word of argument and you'll have just bread and olive oil for supper. And if I ever again hear you speaking to your sister in such foul terms, I will wash your mouth out with lejia.'

Juan left, grimacing threats at his sister when certain Dolores could not see his face. Isabel began to sob.

'Stop snivelling.'

'He hurt my shoulder . . .'

'If you snivel every time a male causes you

181

pain, you will have no time for anything else.' She placed her hands on her hips and glared at Jaime. 'You know where your son learns the filth he speaks in the house, don't you?'

'The other boys.'

'From his father. A man who drinks until he is utterly careless about the appalling example he provides for his poor children.'

'Steady on there!'

'Who destroys their innocence without a moment's remorse because drink has robbed him of every decent emotion.'

'Why are you going on like that? This is my first glass . . .'

'You think me so stupid I'll believe any lie, no matter how preposterous?'

'Will you calm down?'

'But perhaps you are right to laugh at me. After all, I married you.' She swept out of the room and into the kitchen.

Jaime said resentfully: 'She's lucky I'm easy going and didn't tell her something.'

She put her head through the bead curtain. 'And what would your drink-laden words have told me?'

Jaime remained silent.

'More lies, so absurd that not even a five-year-old would believe them?' She withdrew. A moment later, there were sounds from the kitchen of things being banged about.

Jaime drank, then said in a low voice: 'Sweet Mary, but it's good to know there's nothing wrong with her after all!'

*   *   *

It had not been a cheerful meal. Dolores had been so aggressively vigilant that even though the opened bottle of wine had provided the two men with no more than a tumblerful each, they had deemed it prudent not to reach into the side-hoard for another bottle.

As Alvarez ate the last of the baked almonds and banana, he looked at his watch.

'You are in a hurry?' Dolores asked.

He swallowed. 'I have to go out. Work.'

'Indeed. Then you didn't change into a clean shirt because you are meeting someone?'

He never ceased to be astonished by her ability to notice things he would have preferred her not to. 'The shirt I was wearing got dirty during the day.'

'And you shaved for a second time because your beard had grown twice as quickly as usual?'

He reached for his glass, realized it was empty.

'Why are men so stupid?' She looked across the table. 'Isabel, Juan, you may get down.'

They gratefully hurried out of the room.

'Men always hope their lies, however pathetic, will be believed. My husband tells me he has had only the one drink, never realizing, that when I went to answer the phone his glass

183

was empty, when I returned, it was not; my cousin says he has changed his shirt and shaved for a second time as he is in a hurry to leave the house because he has to work—work! Aiee! Since it is men who govern, should we be surprised that all is chaos?'

Alvarez said: 'I've had to arrange to meet someone. For the image of the Cuerpo, I need to look neat and tidy.'

'And is this someone a woman?'

'What does that matter?'

She looked up at the ceiling. 'He asks me, does that matter! Does he think I can have forgotten—though how I wish I could—all the times he has made a ridiculous spectacle of himself by lusting after foreign females young enough to be his daughter instead of having the sense to become friendly with a decent Mallorquin woman of property whose husband has recently died?'

'There's no reason to go on like this. I'm only seeing her because—'

'Then she is a woman!'

'Because she can help me with my investigation.'

'Is she foreign?'

'Yes, but . . .'

'And half your age?'

'That's ridiculous. She may be a little younger . . .'

She stood. 'My cousin is so lost to any sense of shame that he sits in the square, where all can see him, drinking with a woman who is less than half his age and dressed in such a way that decent people avert their gaze!'

'Whoever phoned you earlier obviously didn't avert her gaze. Presumably, she's not decent?'

She held her head high and, lustrous dark brown eyes smouldering, marched through to the kitchen.

'You've really done it,' Jaime said, a note of admiration in his voice.

*　　*　　*

Alvarez turned into the small car park on the front and came to a stop when he saw Phoebe standing by a green Mercedes on the opposite side. The lightest of breezes was stirring loose strands of her hair and these played a desultory tag across her forehead and cheeks; her frock was simple in design, yet it suited her with sophisticated smartness. Discretion and unwitting provocation, he thought. A combination that could well spell danger for a man less mature than himself.

She saw him and came across. He leaned over to open the passenger door and she sat, settling a beach-bag at her feet. 'I'm sorry I'm late,' he said.

'Is it really possible to be late in this country?'

He smiled.

'Where are we going?'

'I wondered if you'd like a drive to the lighthouse and, either before or after, have a drink at the Hotel Parelona?'

'That sounds ideal. Larry was talking about the hotel only yesterday and reckons it really does live up to its name. He also said that after the tourists have left the beach, the swimming's fabulous . . . Have you brought your costume?'

'I'm not a keen swimmer.'

'When you live here? Shame on you!'

The drive, long in time but not in distance, was seldom less than dramatic, with constantly varying views of idyllic bays, glass-smooth sea, monstrous cliffs, and ever more hills.

On the descent towards the hotel, he said: 'We're coming to the point of turning off for the lighthouse. What would you like to do: carry on and come back for a drink, or stop now?'

'Which do you suggest?'

'If we carry on, we can see the sun set; sometimes the sea can look as if it's on fire.'

'That would be a fitting climax to such an exciting drive. We simply can't miss the chance of that. What's more, it'll mean I'll have my swim in the dark, which is twice as much fun because of the mystery.'

There were more questions he had intended surreptitiously to put, but she was so obviously enjoying herself it struck him that to question her tonight would be to mock her naivety. As

186

he changed gear and turned left, he assured himself that his decision had been made on purely professional grounds.

They drove for several kilometres along what had become a nearly level road, then this began to climb once more, passed through a tunnel, and became increasingly tortuous until it finally brought them to the lighthouse, on the tip of the island.

As if to order, the setting sun turned the water a glittering, golden red.

'Wow!' she said.

Hardly a poetic reaction, but not even lines by Felipe Almunia could have pleased him more.

*   *   *

They had two drinks on the gently lit terrace of the hotel, then walked through the gardens to the beach. He sat at the base of a palm tree. He had expected her to move well away to change because there was some moonlight, but she remained where she was. As he looked firmly out to sea, he heard the quick rasp of a zip being unfastened. He tried very hard not to imagine the consequences of that evocative sound . . .

'I love swimming,' she said, 'so I can spend ages in the water without realizing it. When you get bored, give me a shout.'

As she ran across the sand and into the sea,

becoming too indistinct to be more than a moving shadow, he wished himself an Olympic gold medallist, capable of cleaving the water like a torpedo.

*   *   *

He drove into the car park and braked to a halt close to the green Mercedes.

'You've given me an evening to remember for a long, long time,' she said.

'I'm glad,' was all he could find to answer.

She opened the door and stepped out. Belatedly, he left his car to cross with her to the Mercedes. She unlocked, sat behind the wheel, pressed a switch to lower the window. 'Once again, thanks a million.'

The nearest streetlight was sufficiently far away that her face was only partially illuminated; shadows added a touch of intriguing sophistication.

'See you sometime.'

'How about tomorrow evening?' he asked.

'Great!'

CHAPTER TWENTY-ONE

Dolores sighed. As Alvarez cut himself a second slice of coca, she sighed again.

'What's up?' he asked.

'You can ask?'

He realized what the sighs portended. He ate a mouthful of coca and added another spoonful of sugar to the hot chocolate.

'I heard you return last night.'

'I'm sorry. I tried to be quiet.'

'It was after midnight.'

'Was it? I didn't keep an eye on the time.'

'What man does when he loses his wits?'

'Why go on and on like this? I only saw her last night because of work; but for that, I wouldn't have bothered.'

'You think me so stupid as to believe that?'

'I've told you . . .'

'You tell me many things. Only because I am a simple, trusting person do I manage to believe even half of them.'

'There's evidence I have to check and she can help me do that.'

'And in order to do so, it is necessary to spend the whole night with her?'

'All night? You've just told me I was back soon after midnight.'

'I did not say "soon" . . . Enrique, can you not see how it distresses me to know you are going to be hurt once more?'

'Why should I be when I know exactly what I'm doing?'

'When a man says that, he knows less than nothing.' She turned her back on him and banged a few things around.

'You don't understand.'

'My misfortune is that I understand perfectly.'

'It's not like you think. Why won't you listen?'

'Because it is always the same story when an old man meets a young woman.'

'I am not an old man.'

'To her, you are.'

'There are only a few years' difference between us. I promise you . . .'

'Men only make promises when they intend to break them.'

He gave up.

*   *   *

He was thinking that it was nearing time to leave the office when the telephone rang. The caller was Phoebe.

'I'm sorry, Enrique, but I've got to call off our trip this evening.'

'Why?' he said, far more sharply than intended.

'The two maids have the night off and the daily who was supposed to come in and house-sit because Larry and Vera are out to dinner has just rung to say she can't turn up because her husband's ill. Larry doesn't like leaving the place empty and asked me to stay in, not knowing I'd arranged to meet you. The moment he heard that, he said not to worry, but after all their kindness, I feel I can't let

190

them down.'

He had been looking forward to seeing her again and his disappointment was sharp—a disappointment, he hurriedly assured himself, which arose from the fact that a few more artfully hidden questions should provide all the remaining answers he needed. 'I could come and see you at Son Preda if you'd like?'

'To tell the truth, I did think of suggesting that, but then I reckoned it was such a way to have to drive for a boring evening.'

'It's no distance and it couldn't begin to be boring.'

'Ever the diplomat!' She chuckled.

*   *   *

He drew up in front of the house. As he left the car, the front door opened and Phoebe stepped out and unbidden there came into his mind that more than any other woman he'd ever met, she presented the two faces of Eve—fresh innocence and lusty promise.

'I hope you like sitting out for drinks and a snack meal,' she said. 'For me, that's one of the supreme joys of living here. As it gets dark, the air becomes cooler and fresher, the stars are crystal clear, the world hushes . . . You'd have to have lived in England to understand why it's all so special. Come on in. I thought we'd settle by the pool because of the view. I hope you've brought your costume.'

191

'I haven't because I didn't know there was a swimming pool here.'

'Would you have done had you known?'

'Yes,' he answered rashly.

'Then there are several spare costumes and one of them is bound to fit you.'

'That's good,' he said, hoping he sounded more enthusiastic than he felt.

The pool was two hundred metres behind the house and had been sited so that from the open section of the complex a wide arc of the surrounding land was visible.

'I always tell myself that here one can look out at part of the island as it once was—before the tourists arrived.' She came to a stop. 'Is that so?'

'In a way, I suppose it is.'

'But something's very different?'

'In the old days, every field would be under cultivation and there'd be men, women, and older children working in them right up to dark.'

'You love the land, don't you?'

'Yes,' he answered simply.

She went over to one of the cane chairs grouped around the table, and sat. 'Will you be barman? The drinks are inside. I'd love a long gin and tonic, going easy on the gin, with lots of ice. If you can't find what you want for yourself, give me a shout and I'll get it from the house.'

The large, central room in the complex was equipped for casual living and there were gas stove, refrigerator, store cupboards, dining-table and chairs; on two of the walls hung woven squares with primitive designs in bold colours, on the third, four framed prints of Mallorquin scenes; matting covered much of the tiled floor.

He poured out the drinks, added ice and a slice of lemon to her glass, ice to his, returned outside.

She had moved her chair so that she was in the low-angled sunshine and had drawn up her skirt until her legs were fully exposed. He handed her a glass, sat, and tried to concentrate on anything but her legs.

'What are you thinking?' she asked.

He hastily prevaricated. 'That one usually remembers the good and forgets the bad.'

'What's got you dissecting life instead of enjoying it?'

'You asked if looking out at the land was like seeing the past and that made me nostalgic. But I'm quite certain that if I'd been one of those labouring in the fields from dawn to dusk, I'd have been longing for the future.'

'When you couldn't have known the future would be so much better?' She raised her glass. 'No more deep thoughts. I don't like you all serious.' She drank. 'Supper will have to be easy to prepare because I'm only half-domesticated and don't enjoy cooking. Would you like a steak?'

'Very much.'

'Thank goodness. How would you like it?'

'Rare to medium, please.'

'I'll try, but no guarantees . . . It's odd, but when I told Vera you'd be coming here tonight, she began to worry what I could give you to eat because she thought you might be a vegetarian. Heaven knows why. You're much too nice.'

'Are all vegetarians nasty?'

'Of course not. It's just that I always treat vegetarians with caution. Not long ago, Fenella decided to become a vegan and she made life hell for everyone because she became so bad-tempered. Perhaps it was her Frenchman who made her change her mind—if so, he gets my thanks.'

'Her Frenchman?'

'She met him at some literary do in London and was bowled over. Vera was warned by someone that he was a rotter—shades of Tancred—and in a large part that's why she suggested the holiday in Pellapuig; hoped to talk Fenella out of the relationship.'

'Did she succeed?'

'Fenella would probably have refused to believe anything nasty about him just to be bloody-minded, but Neil's sudden appearance and Vera's giving him money made certain of it.'

'Then Señora Dewar still sees this Frenchman?'

'A couple of days ago, friends told Vera over the phone that Fenella had gone to stay in a

Paris hotel. Vera, ever optimistic, rang her there and tried to talk some sense into her. Naturally, the only thanks she got was a vicious request to mind her own business. Fenella then went on to say she was marrying him and was selling up in England and going to live in France.' She drained her glass. 'Vera's been in a state since then, but as I keep saying to her, Fenella's old enough to be left with the consequences of her own mistakes . . . Enough dismal talk. From now on, only cheerful chatter. How about another drink before I get the meal?'

*   *   *

He settled back, a glass of cognac warming in the palm of his hand, and stared into the darkening scene, enjoying an unusual sense of inner contentment.

She broke the silence. 'Is it still the best medical advice to wait for an hour before swimming?'

'I'm afraid I don't know.'

'Since there's no rush, let's assume it is; then when we go in, it'll be dark . . . Why don't you really enjoy swimming?'

'When I was young, there was little or no chance for such things.'

'Was life very hard?'

'My parents had to work the land all possible hours and as soon as I was old enough and not at school, I had to help.'

'Are your parents still alive?'

'They died from broken hearts soon after they were cheated out of their land.'

'Who cheated them?'

'A foreigner who knew its true value.'

'Is it because of them that you're a policeman?'

He said slowly: 'I've asked myself that many times and never found the answer.' He shrugged his shoulders. 'Perhaps we never truly know why we do what we do.'

'So you don't know why you've never married?'

'On the contrary,' he answered bitterly.

'I'm sorry, I should never have said that.'

His mind reached back in time and he saw Juana-María laughing, her eyes bright with love, eager to be his wife and yet slightly fearful because in those days marriage had been a mystery surrounded by myth . . .

She said softly: 'Something awful happened, didn't it?'

'A drunken Frenchman in a car pinned my fiancée against a wall and killed her.'

'You . . . you must curse me for so stupidly reminding you.'

'It happened a long time ago and the years soften everything but themselves.'

'I hope they do,' she said quietly.

*   *   *

196

There was a mirror on the wall of the changing-room and it showed his lily-white flesh to disadvantage. He squared his shoulders and pulled in his stomach, but the difference was not great. He was thankful that she so enjoyed swimming in the dark.

He left the changing-room and walked out on to the pool patio. He could just make out her head at the deep end.

'Jump in,' she called out.

He had seldom felt so ashamed of his fears as then. Prior observation told him the level of water was not more than thirty centimetres below the lip of the pool patio, but because she had not turned on the underwater lights and the moon was behind a puffball of cloud, the drop was dark and his imagination smothered logic and told him it was infinite. Cravenly, he walked to the end of the pool and went down the steps into the warm water.

She swam to where he was, came to her feet. 'We'll race over two lengths.'

'I am a very slow swimmer,' he protested.

'I'll bet you're only saying that to try and gain an unfair advantage. All ready? One, two, three, go.' She began to swim with vigorous skill.

He knew only a laboured breaststroke. His breath shortened, his arms tired, and his heart beat ever faster. As he reached the deep end, he told himself he could swim no further. But,

197

fearing her contempt, he turned and struggled on, finally and breathlessly reaching the shallow end.

She moved through the water to where he stood. 'Loser's forfeit is to stand on your head underwater for twenty seconds.'

'I'm . . .' He choked on the words: too old for that sort of thing. He took as deep a breath as possible and plunged under the surface. As he touched the bottom with his hands, he started to slide sideways and crashed into her. He spluttered to the surface to find her against him so that he could feel the gentle pressure of her barely restrained breasts against his chest. He knew a sudden madness and put his arms around her and kissed her passionately. For a moment, she responded, then she drew apart and he experienced the bitterness of rejection.

'Not yet, Enrique,' she murmured.

His bitterness vanished. Her tone had not been angry, outraged, or amused, it had been soft, warm, appealing to him to be patient—she needed to be certain of her own emotions before willingly acceding to his.

CHAPTER TWENTY-TWO

Alvarez walked into the kitchen. 'What a lovely day! Not a cloud in the sky!'

Dolores, who had been mixing eggs and

flour in a bowl, said sourly: 'Would you expect it to be snowing in August?' She stirred more vigorously. 'There's no coca and I haven't had the time to go out and buy an ensaimada. The bread's stale, but it might make toast. I'm very busy, so if you want some chocolate, you'll have to make it yourself.'

'If you're trying to . . .'

'I am trying to prepare lunch since it is my duty to do so, not because I wish to. Every woman understands the meaning of duty, unlike any man.'

'Last evening I had to . . .'

'It is a matter of indifference to me. Life has taught me that a man will sit at any table which serves the food he craves.'

'I've told you before, it's work.'

'Even though a foreigner, she professes reluctance?'

'Goddamnit . . .'

'Please do not swear in the house.'

The day had temporarily clouded over.

*   *   *

The phone rang at eleven-fifteen on the following Monday. 'The superior chief', said the secretary in her plum-filled voice, 'will speak to you.'

So the strained back was better . . .

'Where the devil's your report?' Salas demanded.

199

'Which report, señor?' Alvarez answered.

'The final one in the Lewis case. A case which, due to mishandling, has cost the department so many pesetas that I am having to explain matters in detail to Madrid who seem unable to appreciate that one man's incompetence could solely be responsible.'

'I haven't been able to send it to you yet.'

'Why the devil not?'

'Because it's only in the last day or so that I've been able to complete my inquiries.'

'Good God, man, weeks ago you admitted you've been chasing shadows.'

'I don't think it's quite that long since I last spoke to you, señor. What has happened is, I decided it was necessary to check the facts by questioning someone who could independently confirm them.'

'It takes you all this time to question one person?'

'It had to be done very subtly.'

'This is hardly the occasion for attempted humour.'

There was a pause. Salas spoke again. 'Well? What have you learned from your "subtle" questioning?'

'That the facts as I had ascertained them are correct.'

'In other words, the entire investigation has been a waste of time and money.'

'I wouldn't say that.'

'Naturally not. However, do not try to gloss

over that fact in your report, which will be on my desk first thing tomorrow morning. Is that perfectly clear?'

'Yes, señor.'

The line went dead.

Alvarez looked at his watch. There was not the time left before lunch to draw up a full report and after his siesta he had arranged to meet Phoebe. The solution, then, was to send a precis, certain that subsequently he would angrily be called upon to enlarge and amend . . .

*   *   *

He leaned back in the chair and raised his legs to rest his heels on some of the unopened mail on his desk. For every man, the world was a constantly changing entity, but for none more so than for him. A month before, life had had nothing special to offer him; now, its horizons were golden . . .

The phone rang.

'Is that you, Enrique?'

He didn't recognize the voice. 'Speaking.'

'Emiliano here. How's life with you?'

'Couldn't be better.' Emiliano who? 'Where are you speaking from—Palma?'

'That's a sour joke! You think we get holidays? I'm in Bitges.'

His mind slipped into gear. Emiliano Calvo, who'd helped him trace Lewis's movements.

'I'm ringing more in hope than belief. We've a case that right now isn't offering us a single lead and I suddenly remembered your visit and wondered whether by some lucky chance your inquiries then could offer us anything now . . . A few days ago, a couple of Germans on holiday were scuba diving roughly a kilometre out from shore when they found a body, weighted down to the bottom by a block of concrete. Because of the state of the body it's impossible to make a direct identification and all the experts can tell us is that it's female, aged somewhere between thirty-five and fifty-five, and death probably occurred between two and six months ago. We've checked all local and national records of missing persons and no woman of the right age and size is listed, which means the odds are she was a foreigner, but there's been no request from abroad for help in tracing such a female. Is there any chance that she could have some connection with the man you were tracking?'

There was a good chance, but because the possibility ringed his heart with ice, he was not yet prepared to admit this. 'Right now, I can't think that there is,' he answered, his voice hoarse.

'It always was one hell of a long shot!' Calvo changed the conversation and discussed Salas at length and in slanderous terms.

When the call was over, Alvarez slumped back in the chair. A man's world could be irretrievably turned upside down by a single telephone call. He struggled to convince himself that he was adding two and two and making five, but the more he tried, the more convinced he became that the total was four.

CHAPTER TWENTY-THREE

'Nothing good ever came from bad,' Dolores said mournfully.

'That's guaranteed to cheer me right up!' Alvarez muttered. 'So what are you expecting—that the plane will crash?'

'How can you be so cruelly stupid?'

'When you say things like that . . .'

'What do you expect me to say when for days you have spent every hour with a woman half your age and now you're taking her to Paris?'

'I've told you a dozen times, she's not half my age, I'm not taking her anywhere, I'm going on my own to Paris to work, and if I had my way, I wouldn't be going.'

She sniffed loudly.

'You don't believe me?'

'I cannot perform miracles.'

He left the house, climbed into his car, fixed the seat belt, and drove off. He reached the edge of the village and continued along the lane which bordered the dry torrente to reach the Palma road. The lights controlling the crossing to the sports centre were set at red and he braked to a halt. Yet again, he mentally checked what he'd done. He'd phoned Calvo in Bitges and asked for a chart of the dead woman's teeth to be sent to England for confirmation of identity; using Salas's name, he'd contacted the Police Judiciaire in Paris and requested their full co-operation, citing urgency as the reason for not going through the usual bureaucratic channels; he'd booked a room in a hotel in Paris, and, because he was desperately trying to fool himself into not accepting what he now was convinced was the truth, he'd told Phoebe he'd not be able to see her that evening, as arranged, because he'd had to travel to Paris in connection with a case which had suddenly cropped up . . .

The lights changed and he drove forward. Dully, he wondered why he was pursuing the truth when only he was in a position to uncover it; were it to remain unknown, he could avoid so much pain. But even as he asked himself the question, he knew the answer. The truth was always so much more important than the individual.

*   *   *

In early September, with the holidays over, Paris had regained its rhythm. Love, the excitement of love, the expectation of love, the illusion of love, the delusion of love, had returned to the streets, the cafés, the restaurants, the cinemas and the theatres; citizens seized every opportunity to express themselves, preferably by a show of curt rudeness towards foreigners.

'I don't understand,' said Commissaire Pensec of the Police Judiciaire.

'I am sorry, monsieur; I fear my French is not very good,' Alvarez said, knowing he was fluent, but his accent not Parisian.

Pensec, with a wave of the right hand, indicated that he was a tolerant man.

'On the twenty-sixth of last month, Madame Fenella Dewar was supposedly staying at a hotel in this city. I need to make certain that she indeed did so.'

'The name of the hotel?'

'I regret I do not know it.'

'You really expect us to check the past occupancy lists of every hotel in Paris?'

'I realize it is a very considerable task, but hopefully it will not prove impossible. I imagine you have long since computerized your records—even we have recently done so.'

This implied acceptance of France's innate superiority in all things was sufficient to secure Pensec's co-operation. 'We like to help our colleagues from other countries whenever it is possible to do so.'

*　　　*　　　*

The telephone call was made at nine-thirty the next morning. 'Inspector Alvarez, from Mallorca?'

'That's me, mademoiselle.' His caller sounded sufficiently school-marmish to remind him of the vinegar-faced woman who had tried to teach him elementary algebra, a subject for which he had ever since felt great dislike.

'I have been instructed to inform you that Madame Dewar stayed for three days at the Hôtel Les Colonnes, Rue Fouleries. This is in the eighth arrondissement. When do you wish to make your inquiries?'

'Right away, if that's in order?'

'Officer Curien will meet you there.'

He left his hotel, hailed a taxi, and was driven to a road that was wide and tree-lined and which possessed an ambience of bourgeois dignity. In keeping with the setting, the hotel was marked only by a small awning, a brass plaque, and a doorman in uniform. The doorman, able to judge a potential tip to the last centime, did not bother to open one of the two glass swing doors for him. The foyer was designer smart, with inlaid reception desk, thick pile carpets, leather covered armchairs, period-style tables, velvet draperies, and paintings neutral both in subject and execution.

He crossed to the reception desk, which was staffed by two men in black jackets. One of them directed him to where a younger man was seated. As he approached, Curien came to his feet. 'Monsieur Alvarez? I'm Pierre.' He had sharp, aggressive features, but his manner was friendly.

'It is a pleasure to meet you,' Alvarez said formally.

'Ditto . . . Before we move, suppose you set the picture for me.' He sat, waited until Alvarez was seated, said: 'All I got from the boss was that you want to question the staff about an English woman who stayed here last month. What's the angle to the questioning?'

'I want to make certain that she was who she claimed to be: Madame Fenella Dewar.'

'No offence meant—after all, your French is a thousand times better than my Spanish—but don't you mean, you want to prove she was not Madame Dewar?'

'No. It is as I said.'

'You have me confused.'

'My superior chief would not be surprised.'

Curien grinned. 'Sounds like all the superiors I've ever suffered . . . OK, so the object is to prove she's who she said she was. I imagine you want to talk to any of the staff who might have had contact with Madame Dewar?'

'That's right.'

'Which means receptionists, porters, chambermaids, restaurant hands—the restaurant here has a fine reputation. If she's a sensible woman, she'll have dined here more than once. We're talking about the end of last month. Memories ought to stretch that far back, but this is a popular hotel and must have a brisk turnover of guests, so you may need a bit of luck to get anything definite.'

They spoke to the deputy manager, who offered them the use of a small room at the rear of the hotel, obviously an overflow store-room, which overlooked the large number of dustbins awaiting collection in the small courtyard below.

The oldest of the receptionists had received Madame Dewar. Naturally, he had not only asked for her passport and noted the details, he had also discreetly checked that she was the person in the photograph.

The doorman could not recall her.

One of the porters said she'd tipped him generously, but that was all he could remember about her.

The chambermaid who looked after room 41 was no longer young, but to judge by her make-up and manner, that fact had escaped her. 'She was on her own. Next after the Germans who were always complaining.'

'Can you describe her?'

'Why d'you want to know?'

'Just answer the question,' Curien snapped.

She looked at him with sharp dislike.

'Did she dress smartly?' Alvarez prompted.

'She was English.' Her tone evoked ill-fitting twinsets. Pressed to answer more fully, she said that Madame Dewar had worn good quality clothes, but had lacked any sense of chic.

'What was the colour of her hair?'

'Blonde,' she answered immediately. 'And with a face that shape, she needed a totally different style.' She explained why. It seemed she was an expert on hairstyles.

'What else can you remember about her?'

She shrugged her shoulders. 'The managers are slave drivers so it's always work, work, and no time to worry about the guests unless they're ill-mannered and complain ... If you want to know more, try asking Héloïse—she's always ready to stand around and chat.'

'Why should she have met Madame Dewar?'

'I was taken ill around that time; can't say for certain, but maybe she did room 41 while the Englishwoman was still there ... The doctor said I was to stay home for five days, but management tried to argue I should be back after three. They'd have us working after we're dead, if they could.'

'Then it's fortunate for the guests that they can't,' said Curien. 'Find Mademoiselle Héloïse and ask her to come here.'

After she'd left the room, Curien said sympathetically: 'Not much luck so far.'

'I'm learning enough,' Alvarez answered.

'You surprise me! ... And forgive me saying so, but if you are, it doesn't seem to bring you much cheer.'

'I was hoping I'd learn nothing.'

'You now confuse me even more! However, one thing I understand, you must become cheerful. When are you returning to Spain?'

'On the first available flight.'

'With your agreement, I will discover that that is not until tomorrow morning. Then tonight we will go to Le Nouveau Petit Chou. I hear that the show makes old men young and young men frantic. If I have a word with . . .' There was a knock on the door. 'Enter,' he called out.

A young woman stepped into the room, stood uneasily just inside the doorway. Round faced, brown-cheeked, the maid's uniform sitting uneasily on a solid frame, she lacked any stylish smartness. Country born and bred, was Alvarez's immediate judgement.

'Shut the door,' said Curien impatiently.

'Sit down and get comfortable,' said Alvarez. When she was seated, he continued: 'I expect you know why we want a word with you—we're hoping you'll be able to tell us something about one of the guests.'

'Madame Dewar?' Already, Alvarez's quiet, friendly manner, in sharp contrast to Curien's, had restored her confidence.

'Can you remember her?'

She nodded.

'Tell us about her.'

She spoke with considerable detail, much of it immaterial, and at one point Curien would have hurried her along but for a quick shake of Alvarez's head. She had reported for work at seven and had been preparing to serve

210

breakfast when Jules had told her that Madeleine had reported sick and she must share Madeleine's duties with Denise. That had meant extra work, but since she'd be paid more, she hadn't minded, she sent as much money home as possible because her father was an invalid and the social allowance was far from generous. She had taken a breakfast of two croissants and coffee into room 41. Madame Dewar had been in bed. Unlike some guests, she'd been friendly and, even though her French had been difficult to understand, they'd chatted for quite a while; Madame Dewar had asked where in France she was from and she'd told her and how difficult things were for her father . . . Madame Dewar had been wearing a kind of a negligee over pyjamas . . .

'What colour was her hair?'

'Blonde. And it looked genuine because there was no darkening at the roots; leastwise, none I could see.'

'Did you speak to her again?'

'When I collected the breakfast tray. She'd dressed and was packing because she was leaving that morning.'

'How was she dressed?'

'Nice, but not smart, if you know what I mean. Not like the lady who was next in the room, with a husband who maybe wasn't her husband. When Madeleine came back to work, she said that that lady really had style, but where I come from, when someone dresses like

211

her, we don't say she's smart, we say she's a . . . It's of no account.'

'When you collected the tray, was that the last time you saw Madame Dewar?'

'That's right. When I went in later to do the room, she'd gone.' She hesitated, then said: 'I don't know why you're asking or what's wrong, monsieur, but she seemed a really nice lady.'

'You don't think she might have been putting on an act?' Alvarez's voice was suddenly bitter.

'I . . . I don't understand,' she said uneasily.

'It's of no account.' He was annoyed with himself for letting his inner feelings briefly surface.

'If she wasn't a really nice person, she wouldn't have left me the note.'

'What note?'

'Saying she was giving me the present to buy something for my father to cheer him up. There's mighty few like that, I can tell you!'

'What was the present?'

'Some money.'

'How much?'

She shrugged her shoulders and her expression became blank.

'Well, how much was it?' Curien demanded.

She did not answer.

'You're meant to put all tips in the pot, I suppose?'

'It's immaterial,' Alvarez said. 'And if it was given to her specifically for her father, then it was not for sharing.' He turned. 'Thank you,

212

mademoiselle. And I hope the present gave your father much pleasure.'

She gave him a brief smile of gratitude for his understanding, left.

'That's the last of the staff,' Curien said.

Alvarez nodded.

'So was she Madame Dewar?'

'Undoubtedly,' he answered sadly.

'Then shall we arrange things for an evening at Le Nouveau Petit Chou?'

He thought it would be much more in keeping with his present mood to arrange to spend the night on a bed of thorns, but accepted that Curien's proposal was the more sensible.

CHAPTER TWENTY-FOUR

The stewardess brought him a second brandy and, as she handed him the glass, he was certain she was trying to judge whether he might cause trouble before the end of the flight. She need not have worried. If a man drank to forget, he remembered; if to overcome inner pain, the pain increased.

How did the saying go? A man in love was always betrayed, if not by his lover then by himself. He recalled how, worried by the duplicity, he had almost baulked at using Phoebe as an unwitting source of the truth.

How she must secretly have been laughing at him . . . Of course, he'd been stupid long before she'd been introduced to the scene to make a complete fool of him. Once he'd identified blackmail as a likely motive, he should have realized what was at stake—any man of reasonable intelligence would have done . . .

Clough—personable, amusing, smart, an entrepreneur and exposing just that suggestion of amorality which intrigued, but did not warn—had successfully pursued both profit and women. But then, as had many others, he'd been caught out by changing financial conditions and had found himself in growing financial trouble. The banks, always eager to lift those who were on their way up and kick those who were on their way down, became ever more demanding and threatened to bankrupt his business. To be seen to fail would be almost as painful as the actual failure. He had followed a well-worn path and set out to marry a woman whose attraction was not physical or emotional, but wealth.

It had been a dull marriage and he'd continued to search for, and find, excitement with other women. For a time, Vera had not suspected because it was her nature to trust. He'd wanted to buy more land, convinced that this would enable him to climb out of his financial problems, and she had agreed to offer further surety. Then she'd learned that he had been messing about with another woman and had withdrawn her agreement, only to listen to his denials of adultery and reinstate it . . .

At this point, the course of events became uncertain. Had he been having an affair which had turned his thoughts to murder; or had he already been contemplating it, even if more as a daydream than a real possibility? Had he been having an affair with Fenella, so similar in looks yet so different in character, because she was Vera's sister and this afforded him perverse satisfaction; or, having decided on murder, had he evolved a plan that called on Fenella to play a major part in it and then pursued her, using every ounce of charm and cunning to persuade her to join him?

Not, of course, that Fenella would have needed all that much persuading. Life had turned very sour for her, while for her sister it had become ever sweeter (in her world, husbands were superfluous). Added to which, Vera was always seeking to help and little bred a more positive hatred than the sense of being beholden to someone of whom one was intensely jealous. So when Clough had proposed a move that would benefit both of them, she had not rejected the idea with horror, but had agreed to co-operate.

Clough had recognized the biggest problem of any murder—what to do with the body? Both its presence and its absence could become a voice from the grave. So what surer way of overcoming the problem than to make it

215

appear there had been no murder? The two sisters were alike in looks, except for the colour of their hair, and very dissimilar in character; hair could be dyed and restyled, a false character could be assumed. No one would wonder what had happened to Fenella if she had made it known that she'd fallen in love with a Frenchman and was going to live with him in France. Of course, those who knew Vera even moderately well would not be fooled for long if face-to-face with Fenella, so Fenella and Clough would have to live abroad and contact with Vera's friends would be restricted to letters or phone calls on an ever-diminishing scale; should any of them propose a visit, good reasons would be found to postpone this until the person concerned accepted that Vera had found a new life and didn't wish to maintain contact with the old one. Her financial assets would be transferred to an offshore base and since the advisers would be dealing with Fenella from the word go, they would never have cause to question her authority.

Clearly, if the murder took place abroad, there was a better chance of consolidating the switch of identities. The house in Pellapuig was nigh perfect for the murder—it wasn't overlooked and the cliff was high enough to ensure that Vera must be killed on the rocks below . . . Perhaps it was only at this point of the planning that Clough had recognized a problem. There was little or no tide in the Mediterranean and few strong currents, so if Vera's body was left where it fell there had to be every chance it would be discovered before decomposition made identification virtually impossible. It must be taken out to sea, weighted, and sunk. He could do that, of course, but because fate so often made a mockery of certainty, he had to allow for the fact that it might become necessary for him to prove he was nowhere near his wife when she died to his great benefit. This raised a further problem. The hired accomplice might, after dumping the body, decide to try blackmail. In which case, he would have to be paid whilst plans were made for his murder . . .

Fenella had rented the house in Pellapuig. It had been planned that Clough, ever the loving husband, should join Vera there for a few days, but when he arrived it was to find that Vera had not. Whilst he and Fenella were on their own, he'd made the mistake of sharing her bed, probably at her insistence, never stopping to think that the maid might have sufficient intelligence to realize what was going on . . .

Fenella had received her sister with hypocritical affection. Vera would have been so gratified by this that it would not have occurred to her to wonder what had brought about Fenella's conversion on the road to Pellapuig. Her belief in the eventual triumph of goodness over evil made her a natural victim.

One evening after dark, Fenella had drugged the drink she had given Vera and very soon Vera had become comatose. Fenella must have found it very difficult to lift Vera out of the chair and drag her to the rails of the patio, then to tip her over. Had the physical effort helped her to blank her mind to the actuality of what she was doing? Or had hatred and jealousy long since strangled the last vestige of conscience? Lewis had been waiting, probably in an inflatable, and he had sailed out to sea, weighted the body, tipped it over the side.

As Clough had foreseen, Lewis had decided he'd been given a passport to an easy life. A traditionalist, when he'd demanded a million pesetas as the price of keeping his mouth shut, he would have promised this to be the first and last time. Clough would silently have agreed.

Lewis's death was to be an 'accident'. This was made very much easier by his having extravagantly chartered a motor cruiser because it helped in the pursuit of women. Every year, people fell overboard and drowned, often when tight; such a death seldom aroused even the slightest suspicion. Clough had watched and waited. He'd seen Lewis and Sheard pick up Kirsty and Cara and settle in a café, had quickly boarded the *Aventura* and drugged the full bottle of whisky. When they'd sailed out of port, he'd followed them in his own boat and anchored close to where they'd anchored. Once all aboard the

Aventura was quiet, he'd swum across and boarded, little suspecting that Kirsty was not completely unconscious. He'd exchanged the bottles and glasses, pushed Lewis over the stern, bruising him in doing so, then held him underwater until he'd drowned.

He had overlooked Sheard. There were Sheards in every Mediterranean tourist centre, cunning, amoral, doing as little real work as possible. Sheard had probably surprised himself when he'd befriended Lewis. If so, he'd have seen it as a just reward when Lewis suddenly had money to spend, because instinct, experience, and common sense all suggested this wealth had in some way to be illegal and therefore might be a source of profit for him as well. At some point, he'd learned that Lewis was in contact with Clough—perhaps when Kirsty had heard the reference to Larry—and, after Lewis's death, he'd set out to turn that knowledge into profit. Basically a very stupid man, he'd never foreseen that in doing this he might easily become the victim of another 'accident'.

Guilt could make even the most self-confident man fear danger where, in fact, none existed; a casual remark could bear a meaning never intended by the speaker, a joke could become a threat, silence an accusation. As the inquiries into Lewis's death, and then Sheard's, continued, Clough had begun to fear that however incompetent the investigation, a

219

corner of the truth might become lifted. So he had decided that the best way of averting such danger was to introduce someone who would, apparently guilelessly, confirm all he'd said . . .

Any man could lose his wits to wine and woman; the lucky one lost his only to wine. Phoebe had earned every peseta or pound she had been paid. With professional skill, she'd set out to capture his affections, thus ensuring that while he shamefacedly set out to question her without her suspecting, in truth she had fed him the lies that Clough had paid her to . . .

A jolting thump scattered his thoughts and jerked him back to the present to find they had landed, undercarriage, wings, and engines still attached. It seemed suitably ironic that his bitter thoughts should have saved him from the terrors of the landing.

CHAPTER TWENTY-FIVE

Dolores hugged Alvarez, then released him. 'How are you?'

'All right.'

Jaime, standing by her side in the front room, said: 'She's done nothing but worry about you. Can't think why!'

'Because you are incapable of thinking about anyone but yourself,' she snapped. She spoke once more to Alvarez. 'I've cooked you Llom amb col for supper.'

'That's great,' he answered dully. He picked up his suitcase. 'I'll go up to my room and unpack.'

'Never mind that. Have a drink to celebrate your return.'

'And another to celebrate your arrival,' suggested Jaime.

She swung round. 'Can you talk nothing but stupidities?'

'Here, why d'you keep going on and on at me?'

'Because you should realize that Enrique is too exhausted to have to listen to nonsense.'

'Exhausted, is he? Been enjoying himself too much in gay Paree!'

She made a sound of sharp annoyance, crossed to the inner doorway, then came to a stop. 'Before I forget, there was a phone call from Palma. You're to ring back as soon as possible.'

Life, Alvarez thought, enjoyed trampling with hobnail boots on a man who was already done. 'How did the superior chief sound—even worse than usual?'

'It wasn't him, but someone called Amengual from the Institute of Forensic Anatomy. You can ring now; it'll be some time before supper's on the table.'

He stared at the telephone as they left. Why bother to ring Palma and learn what he already knew—that he had been an utter fool?

221

Nevertheless, he dialled the Institute's number and asked to be connected with Amengual.

'We've heard from England regarding the dentist's chart you arranged to have sent to them. They managed to identify Señora Clough's dentist who provided a chart of her teeth for comparison. There's no match.'

He couldn't make sense of that. 'There has to be.'

'They say not.'

'Then they've made a mistake.'

'The report's too definite for that.'

If the dead woman was not Vera Clough, then she was an unknown victim which meant that his whole reconstruction of events on the island and in Pellapuig crumbled into dust. Señora Clough was alive and well and living in Son Preda. Phoebe had not been paid to fool him into believing lies. And when she had murmured 'Not yet', he had read the truth in her words. The room was suddenly filled with sunshine even though it faced north.

He laughed as he replaced the receiver. The joys of being wrong; the pleasures of being proved incompetent! Because he had believed Phoebe a bitch, he had bought her nothing in Paris. Now he could be certain she was not, it became imperative to give her a present. (Guiltily, he accepted that in part this was to salve his own conscience.) Then she should have the one intended for Dolores and somehow he'd make it up to Dolores . . .

He whistled as he went through to the dining-room.

'What's up with you?' Jaime asked.

He poured himself a drink, raised his glass. 'Tonight, I drink with the gods.'

'If you ask me, you've been doing that all the way back from France.'

Alvarez laughed, whistled a few bars from 'Viva España', drank.

*   *   *

Alvarez left his car, crossed to the front door of Son Preda and struck the knocker a resounding blow. In his right trouser pocket was a gift-wrapped miniature model of the Eiffel Tower in silver. It certainly was not what he would have chosen for Phoebe, but he could be certain that she would treasure it because he had given it to her. The door was opened by the older maid.

'I've come to see Señorita Owen,' he said.

'She's not here.'

The evening was becoming late so she'd soon be back. 'I'll wait.' He stepped inside.

'I'll tell the señor.'

As he waited, he pictured Phoebe's return. First, the rising sound of the approaching car, the slam of a door, the crunch of her feet on the gravel surface. Then, surprised, she'd come face to face with him . . .

Clough entered the hall. 'I understand you

want to see Phoebe?' His manner was cold.

'That's right, señor. The maid said she wasn't here, but I imagine she'll be back before long.'

'She's in England.'

His disappointment was immediate and bitter. 'When did she leave?'

'At the weekend.'

'Where's she gone?'

'As I've just said, England.'

'Yes, of course, but I meant where in England? Perhaps you'd be kind enough to give me her telephone number?'

'When she left, she had no idea where she'd be staying.'

'Then how can I get in touch with her?'

'I've no idea.'

Bewildered, Alvarez said; 'Did she leave a message for me?'

'No.'

'Are you sure?'

'Of course.'

Vera looked out from one of the rooms. 'Larry, she did leave the inspector a note.'

He swung round.

'She asked me to give it to him when he returned from Paris.'

'I told her . . .' He stopped abruptly.

'I'll get it for you, Inspector,' she said. She disappeared into the room. Clough, his expression furious, followed her.

Alvarez heard a murmur of voices too low for him to understand what was being said, but the tone in which the words were spoken made it clear they were arguing bitterly. After a while, Vera, her face flushed, returned alone to the hall. She held out an envelope.

'I hope . . .' She shook her head, did not finish.

He thanked her, said goodbye, left. He drove down the dirt track until the headlights picked out the tarmac road, came to a stop. He switched on the interior light, opened the envelope, pulled out the single sheet of paper, read.

'I'm desperately sorry it's got to end like this because I know you'll be hurt and you've told me how much life has hurt you in the past. Try to remember all the fun times we've had, not the way it's ended. P.'

No address. No suggestion of a future. All too clearly, a final goodbye. She'd been so right. He felt as if the hurt were fatal . . .

He drove on to the road and headed for home. Seven minutes later, he braked the car to a halt as confusing thoughts suddenly began to race through his mind. Her note was affectionate. There could be no doubting that. If she had affection for him, why hadn't she waited for his return so that she could explain things in person? If circumstances had suddenly arisen which made this impossible, why hadn't she explained in the note what these were? It was as if she'd written it in a tearing hurry. Could this have been because there was someone who had ordered her to leave silently and quickly and she'd had so little chance to defy the order? . . . Clough's manner back at the house had made it obvious that he'd not known about the note; the muffled, angry argument between him and his wife suggested he'd been trying very hard to prevent her handing it over—she, intensely determined when she needed to be, had insisted . . .

A false character could be assumed with considerable success, but the true, inner character was very difficult to hide. What had he learned about the true characters of the two sisters? Fenella—selfish, resentful, bitterly jealous; Vera—warm-hearted, loyal, generous. The maid in the villa at Pellapuig had found a twenty-thousand-peseta tip in Vera's room. Would anyone set out a tip until just before leaving? It was perhaps conceivable that someone with a very faulty memory might do so in order not to forget, but there was no evidence that Vera had a poor memory . . . In Paris, Fenella had given the chambermaid what had obviously been a considerable gift because she'd been touched by learning about her father's illness . . .

He now knew he'd been right . . . until he'd been wrong.

Clough—ever more bitter and frustrated because his wife had made it obvious, when she'd briefly reneged on her agreement to stand surety for him, that if she ever had proof he was being unfaithful to her, she would cut him out of her life of luxury—had decided to murder her and so gain her fortune. The plan had been straightforward. Vera was to be thrown to her death, Fenella would take her place. But Clough had not known about, and therefore could not warn Fenella against, the possible side effects of the modified chloral hydrate. When it had seemed Vera was unconscious, Fenella had started to drag her towards the edge of the patio. At which point, Vera had gone berserk and, by chance, not intention, forced Fenella over the edge to her death before collapsing into unconsciousness. Lewis had collected the body, never realizing it was the wrong one . . .

When Vera had recovered consciousness sufficiently to realize what had happened, she'd panicked and in desperation telephoned her husband for help. Shocked to hear she was still alive, initially he must have been terrified she was going to accuse him of trying to murder her, but then he'd realized that she suspected nothing and was consumed by fear and guilt; ironically, the failure of his plan could lead to the fulfilment of his ambitions. Fenella had played to perfection the part of a sister welcoming reconciliation, so he could remain the ever-loving husband determined to save his wife. He'd told Vera that she'd obviously suffered some kind of brainstorm and therefore was without the guilt of intention, but in a foreign country it could be almost impossible to persuade the law of her innocence. However, since Fenella's body had fallen into the sea, it was very unlikely ever to be found; even if it were, identification would not be made because no one would know Fenella was missing (thanks, as he naturally did not explain, to the arrangements made for Vera's murder) . . .

Terrified, tortured by conscience and remorse, needing his constant reassurance that she had no reason to blame herself for her sister's death, convinced that she must do exactly as he said because he was trying to save her, Vera had been putty in his hands. She had allowed herself to question nothing; whatever he said was the truth. It was just possible that in a masochistic way she had been grateful for the chance to stifle her common sense . . . And when told to travel to Paris to further the lie, she had seen this as nothing other than self-preservation . . .

As the investigation had dragged on, Clough had begun nervously to wonder if it were just possible that the bumbling Mallorquin detective might stumble on something incriminating. (Would he have been so worried if he had learned how long it had taken to appreciate the significance of the lack of any forensic traces on the bottles and glasses from the *Aventura*?) So he'd paid Phoebe to come to the island to bolster his evidence in a subtle way, guaranteed not to arouse suspicion, and he'd forced Vera to impersonate Fenella in Paris so that no matter what happened, Fenella's death in June would not be suspected. These would have been master strokes had not Fenella's body been discovered by scuba divers. Even then he, Alvarez, had believed that the woman who had stayed in the Paris hotel had been Fenella—until Clough had made the mistake of ordering Phoebe to leave (worried that perhaps she was becoming too emotionally sympathetic?) so abruptly that she had written a note to try to belie the curt insensitivity of her silent departure. Finally, had Vera's nature not been so sentimental that she had refused her husband's demands to tear up the note . . .

Alvarez engaged first gear and drove off. He had cause for pride. Because he had finally uncovered the truth, he could free Vera from the mental torture to which she had been subjected. He could also ensure that Clough did not have the chance once again to plan her murder, thereby finally getting his hands on her fortune. But all this at what pain to himself?

*   *   *

He entered the house and carried on through to the dining-room where he brought a bottle of brandy and a glass out of the sideboard. He poured himself a drink, went through to the kitchen for ice. When he returned, Dolores,

229

wearing a dressing-gown over a lace-edged nightdress, stood in the far doorway. 'Do you have to swill down still more drink?' she demanded angrily.

'Yes,' he replied simply.

Her expression changed to one of concern. 'I thought when you left here . . .' She stopped.

'So did I.'

She sat on the nearest chair. 'It was so wonderful to see you smile and hear you whistle and sing . . . I need a drink.'

He went back into the kitchen for water, brought a glass out of the sideboard, poured into it a generous brandy, added water and ice, passed it to her. He drained his glass, refilled it. Slowly, a little of the pain lifted. By writing him that note in sharp defiance of Clough's orders, Phoebe was telling him that while initially her affection had been bought, soon it had become a willing gift . . .

There was a shout from the stairs. 'Where are you? What's going on?'

Jaime appeared in the doorway, tousle-haired and wearing only pyjama trousers. 'Well, bury me tomorrow if you're not both boozing! Happy days!' He hurried forward to the sideboard.

We hope you have enjoyed this Large Print book. Other Chivers Press or Thorndike Press Large Print books are available at your library or directly from the publishers.

For more information about current and forthcoming titles, please call or write, without obligation, to:

Chivers Press Limited
Windsor Bridge Road
Bath BA2 3AX
England
Tel. (01225) 335336

OR

Thorndike Press
P.O. Box 159
Thorndike, Maine 04986
USA
Tel. (800) 223-2336

All our Large Print titles are designed for easy reading, and all our books are made to last.